GENOCIDAL LOVE

"Intimate and unflinching, *Genocidal Love* lays bare how residential school violence lingers in the body, eating away at lives and communities. Yet, in her vividly resilient portrayal of Myrtle, Bevann Fox tears beauty from the jaws of genocide, daring to claim love beyond settler imaginings—love that nurtures decolonial futures and makes possible a more just world. This book is an act of defiant generosity."

—Sam McKegney, author of *Magic Weapons* and *Masculindians*

"This is a gem of a book.... Indian women need to read this, and so do settlers/newcomers. Bevann Fox offers a unique contribution to the body of Indian residential school literature. I cannot think of another recent text that ruminates on the effects of residential schools on romantic partnerships from a woman's perspective."

—Michelle Coupal, Canada Research Chair in Truth, Reconciliation, and Indigenous Literatures

"*Genocidal Love* by Bevann Fox is a riveting, often difficult, brave, important book about an outspoken little girl living in a boisterous, loving family on reserve, who is sent to residential school where she is abused, humiliated, and left unable to articulate the damage done to her. As an adult she examines the long-lasting genocidal effects that linger and resonate in her life, even as she searches for a way to unlearn the lessons of self-hatred taught to her. This book reveals the trauma in calling the State and Church to account and the pain a generation of residential school survivors experienced when bringing the truth of abuse to light. It also celebrates the possibilities of healing."

—Deanna Reder, Chair, Department of Indigenous Studies, Simon Fraser University

"A riveting and courageous reflection of the author's abusive experience at residential school, *Genocidal Love* is unique in its detailed account of the often re-traumatizing effects of the legal and bureaucratic barriers of compensation programs predating the Truth and Reconciliation Commission."

—Jesse Rae Archibald-Barber, editor of *kisiskâciwan* and co-editor of *Performing Turtle Island*

GENOCIDAL LOVE

A Life After Residential School

BEVANN FOX

Printed and bound in Canada at Imprimerie Gauvin. The text of this book is printed on 100% post-consumer recycled paper with earth-friendly vegetable-based inks.

Cover art: "Hair cut off on the floor isolated on white background," by Pakawat/Adobe Stock.
Cover design: Duncan Campbell, University of Regina Press
Interior design: John van der Woude, JVDW Designs
Copy editor: Kendra Ward
Proofreader: Rhonda Kronyk
Discussion questions contributed by Michelle Coupal with the generous help of a SSHRC grant.

Library and Archives Canada Cataloguing in Publication

Title: Genocidal love : a life after residential school / Bevann Fox.
Other titles: Abstract love
Names: Fox, Bevann, 1968- author.
Description: Previously published under title: Abstract love.
Identifiers: Canadiana (print) 20200238183 | Canadiana (ebook) 20200238434 | ISBN 9780889777415 (softcover) | ISBN 9780889777477 (hardcover) | ISBN 9780889777439 (PDF) | ISBN 9780889777453 (EPUB)
Subjects: LCSH: Fox, Bevann, 1968-—Childhood and youth—Fiction. | LCSH: Indigenous children—Abuse of—Canada—Fiction. | CSH: Native peoples—Canada—Residential schools—Fiction. | LCGFT: Creative nonfiction. | LCGFT: Autobiographies.
Classification: LCC PS8611.O9 A63 2020 | DDC C813/.6—dc23

10 9 8 7 6 5 4 3 2

University of Regina Press, University of Regina
Regina, Saskatchewan, Canada, S4S 0A2
TEL: (306) 585-4758 FAX: (306) 585-4699
WEB: www.uofrpress.ca

We acknowledge the support of the Canada Council for the Arts for our publishing program. We acknowledge the financial support of the Government of Canada. / Nous reconnaissons l'appui financier du gouvernement du Canada. This publication was made possible with support from Creative Saskatchewan's Book Publishing Production Grant Program.

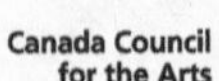

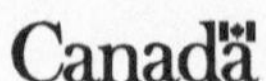

In memory of my late grandfather, Gaston Anaskan, Nimosōmipan, for his inspiration. He said, "One day you will write a book." Also to my beautiful grandmother, Myrtle Anaskan, Nohkōmipan.

Content Warning

This book may bring awareness and rekindle memories. Although some parts may hurt, other parts may help move you through energies unsettled within you or that may have been asleep until now. My intent is not to hurt anyone but to bring back something lost. As I read the book over and over, I cried, laughed, or felt very happy. It has helped me understand more of who I am and helped me release emotions still stored in my body.

So if you find yourself feeling angry, sad, or happy, then embrace that energy, for you are a success. Honour yourself, find some quiet time, make a cup of hot tea, and enjoy reading this book. It is a story about Myrtle, and she wants to share everything with you.

—Bevann Fox

*This story is based on real events.
Names and identifying details have been
changed to protect the privacy of individuals.*

Abstract Life Me

If you can't read the book then wear my abstract shirt
Feel my energy and feel the beauty
A red child living in genocidal love
Please love my freckles
This is an abstract way of life
There is no normal or consistent
There is but constant abstract
As colonialist hands touch everywhere
A seed planted in the mind already
A pattern of abstract love
Of a different life

The red child…
Genocidal love
Love my freckles please…
I have freckles… Just like you.

—Paquahsimou Piyesiw Iskwew
(Raindance Lodge ThunderBird Woman)

CONTENTS

FOREWORD

by MICHELLE COUPAL

I am deeply humbled and honoured by the invitation from Bevann Fox and University of Regina Press to write this foreword to *Genocidal Love.* They asked me to frame and contextualize the incredible story that Bevann has written within the broader body of work that is now known as Indian Residential School literature. I think they approached me because of my scholarly expertise in Indigenous literatures. What they did not know is that my personal story shares some important similarities with the story Bevann tells about her protagonist, Myrtle.

I did not attend residential school, so the setting is different. But like Myrtle, I was held captive between grades one and three by my Uncle, a Catholic Brother, who "took care of me" in the basement of my family home. His three-year reign of terror was made possible by the neglect of my mother and the absence of my father. My Uncle told me that if I ever told anyone what he was doing to me, he would take me to a place where no one would find me. He had a gun, he said, that he would use to kill me if I uttered a word. So, like Myrtle, I lost my voice. I rarely spoke for three years. I was ultimately sent to a speech pathologist, who found nothing wrong with my ability to speak, except that when forced to mouth words I spoke so quietly that it was difficult to hear me. I deliberately muffled my words to make them hard to discern. To this day, I have to concentrate to articulate my words clearly. When I am having difficulty, it sounds like I have slight lisp—the disarticulated cry of a child.

There are many other similarities in our stories—traumatic dissociation, PTSD, and difficulty finding healthy adult relationships with men, to name a few. We share, too, the incredible strength and fortitude that comes with survival, a learned, quiet resilience in the face of new traumas (even if the cracks reopen deeper and wider), and successful careers later in life. We both love to laugh. But, of course, there are many differences. Our stories are our own to tell and in our own time. For survivors of Indian residential school, these are some of the most difficult stories to write and to share. These stories are also difficult to read. Yet they are much more than stories of horrific childhood experiences of sanctioned genocide by the government. These are stories of reconnection, healing, joy, laughter, resistance, strength, and courage.

Genocidal Love contributes to a significant body of work—memoir, fiction, poetry, picture books, graphic novels—written by survivors or family members of survivors about their experiences of Indian residential schools and their ongoing legacies. Indian residential school literature has flourished, especially during and following the work of the Truth and Reconciliation Commission of Canada (TRC). There is enough of it now to call it, as Renate Eigenbrod did as early as 2012, a sub-genre of Indigenous literatures in Canada. The first published memoir of residential schooling in Canada was Jane Willis's, *Geniesh* (1973). That was also the year that Maria Campbell published *Halfbreed,* a pathbreaking autobiography that many scholars cite as marking the beginning of contemporary Indigenous literatures in Canada. Campbell spent one year at a residential school, which she describes briefly but powerfully in *Halfbreed.* The 1970s also saw the publication of Alice French's *My Name is Masak* (1976) and George Kenney's *Indians Don't Cry* (1977).

However, the most famous early memoir published about residential schooling was Basil H. Johnston's *Indian Schools Days* (1986). Johnston wrote the memoir predominantly for his friends who also attended the Spanish Indian Residential School in Ontario. Like the memoirs of the 1970s, Johnston's memoir carefully stories the day-to-day experience of attending the school. He leaves little doubt about the poor quality of education, food, "instruments of suppression" such as bells, gongs, whistles, and clappers (43), and the prison-like environs:

> Our sole aspiration was to be rescued or released (it didn't much matter which) from Spanish, and to be restored to

> our families and homes. That was the sum total of our ambitions. Our vision did not extend beyond the horizon; our world was confined to the playground and the west wing of the building enclosed by fences and walls. The outer world and events taking place therein were as distant and as alien as Mars. The future was tomorrow; beyond that we could not see. (53)

The accounts of residential schooling in these earlier works tend to be less graphic than present-day narratives in chronicling the abuses suffered by the children. Indeed, Basil Johnston waited until he wrote the Foreword to Sam McKegney's *Magic Weapons* (2007) to publicly reveal the sexual abuse he suffered at Spanish. Child sexual abuse remains one of the most difficult and emotionally risky traumas to speak aloud. I was in my late thirties when I started speaking to my family members and friends about my childhood sexual abuse. The decision to do so was complicated. I was motivated by the desire to stop what I perceived to be a false family rhetoric of harmony that placed my mother on a pedestal, with me as the scapegoat who allowed her to stay there. Some of my family members judged me and questioned the veracity of my story. Others didn't blink, as if the fact of it had always been apparent. My judges asked, "How could your mother expose you to a man she knew to be violent and sexually deviant?" And, "How could she *not* tell anyone when she discovered her brother in the act of committing a crime?" These questions came with little thought to my mother's life-long struggle with mental illness, anger, and untreated issues stemming from her own history of child abuse.

I want to address the questions of the judges: "Is she lying?" and "How can such horrific abuse against children happen in a 'civil' society?" Settler-colonial racism and the dehumanizing of Indigenous Peoples tell part of the story, to be sure. It should be remembered that, until fairly recently, there was a culture of institutional abuse in this country. The last residential school did not close its doors until 1996. Corporal punishment was a common occurrence in Canadian public schools and at home in the nineteenth and twentieth centuries. The strap, for example, was not banned in Canada until 2004. And it took until the late 1970s—through the work of second-wave feminists—for child sexual abuse to be recognized as a serious problem in Canada. The many difficulties and reprisals associated with talking about sexual abuse are what allow it to continue to fester. Child sexual abuse lives and breathes in silence.

Speaking out of the silence is a terrifying, gut-wrenching experience. Because children feel implicated in their abuse, it feels shameful to talk about it. When I was a child, no one spoke about sexual abuse. In fact, severe forms of child abuse were not part of circulating public discourses in Canada until the late 1980s. The watershed moment that started a national conversation about institutional child abuse was the 1989 media reports of severe physical and sexual abuses of boys over decades at the Mount Cashel Orphanage in St. John's, Newfoundland. This was closely followed by Phil Fontaine's disclosure in 1990 that he was physically and sexually abused at residential school. The CBC reported thirty years ago that Fontaine, then the head of the Assembly of Manitoba Chiefs, "stunned the nation with his testimony." It is difficult to imagine in our post-TRC age that the abuses suffered at residential school were not widely known outside of Indigenous communities. Yet within communities, too, many survivors did not discuss their abuse, and to this day there are survivors of the schools who are not able to talk about what happened to them. It is simply too painful.

Following Phil Fontaine's public disclosure, there were a series of residential school narratives written and, in the case of plays, performed—notably, by women. Shirley Cheechoo's play, *Path with No Moccasins*, premiered in 1991. Vera Manuel's *Strength of Indian Women* debuted in 1992. That year also saw the publication of Shirley Sterling's fictional autobiography *My Name Is Seepeetza*. What was not known until the recent publication of *Honouring the Strength of Indian Women: Plays, Stories, Poetry* by Vera Manuel (2019), is that before Phil Fontaine's disclosure and before the abuses of Mount Cashel were revealed, Vera Manuel was writing fictionalized stories of the abuses her family suffered at residential schools, including the legacies of the schools that were passed on from generation to generation. These three women writers chose fictional forms to share personal stories of residential schooling, thus paving the way for a series of semi-autobiographical or autobiographical fictions that followed, including Bevann Fox's *Genocidal Love*.

The 1996 release of the final report of the Royal Commission on Aboriginal Peoples (RCAP) coincided with two major publications focussed on residential schooling: Tomson Highway's *Kiss of the Fur Queen* and Rita Joe's *Song of Rita Joe*. The final report of the TRC is in many ways a reiteration of the final report of RCAP, although the focus of the TRC was narrower. RCAP was a robust attempt to bring the devastating consequences of hundreds of years of assimilative government legislation to the national consciousness by asking this central question: "What are the foundations of a fair and honourable relationship between the Aboriginal and non-Aboriginal people of Canada?" This happened in tandem with the rise in prominence of Indigenous writing (not just about residential schools) in Canada. I do not mean to suggest that RCAP is responsible for what has been referred to as a renaissance in Indigenous literature. What I am suggesting is that conversations, whether through creative writing, scholarly work, or public discourse, were raising awareness of the legacies of government legislation aimed to claim land and resources and to destroy Indigenous languages, cultures, and kinship systems. RCAP ultimately lost momentum, for many reasons, including political neglect.

Still, the work of the commission led to the 1998 Statement of Reconciliation by Jane Stewart on behalf of the Government of Canada. This statement included $350 million in funding to launch the Aboriginal Healing Foundation. Community-driven and community-focussed, this foundation saw its good work come to an abrupt conclusion in 2010 when the Conservative government, under the leadership of Stephen Harper, cut its funding (only two years after he issued the formal government apology for residential schools). This decisive moment bears remembrance in the wake of the TRC, which could conclude, as rcap did, as a mostly unremembered past historical event. This is but one of the reasons that residential school literature should continue to be taught and read.

One of the more important yet underread and under-studied contributions to residential school literature is Robert Arthur Alexie's novel, *Porcupines and China Dolls* (2002, 2009). Alexie called his novel "semi-autobiographical," so he employed a similar form to *Genocidal Love*. The choice of authors to use fictional forms to tell their stories is a phenomenon that continues to this day, although non-fictional memoirs appear to be the medium of choice in the post-TRC proliferation of residential school narratives. Fictional autobiographical accounts of residential school experiences allow authors to narrate complex experiences outside of the constraints of public forms of testimony. The form also allows a narrative distance not afforded in memoirs. In a contribution to *Indian Country Today*, Robert Alexie writes a third-person article about a man named Robert, confessing at the end, "Robert is me, or I am Robert. And sometimes he finds it better to write in the third person." In fact, Bevann Fox's earlier version of this novel, *Abstract Love* (2011), was also written in the third person, perhaps for similar reasons.

Fictional autobiography is a Western term. I was curious if there was a Cree word for the genre. Cree-Métis scholar Deanna Reder explained to me in an email that "The categories of fiction and non-fiction don't really work in Cree, not because there isn't an understanding that some things are true and some things are not, but that someone telling their own story might elaborate to make the story more entertaining, and that since everyone tells the story from their own perspective, how one person relates an event might very well differ from someone else's version." She offered the word âcimisowin: a story about oneself. I think this is a helpful way to think about *Genocidal Love*—a story that Bevann tells about herself outside of the boundaries of what constitutes fiction and non-fiction.

The story that Bevann tells about herself is a unique contribution to the existing body of residential school literature in a number of ways. Fictions and memoirs of residential schooling tend to follow a pattern of recounting life before, during, and after the schools, with the bulk of the narrative focussed on life during and after the schools—loveless institutions, essentially prisons, that sought to acculturate inmates into dominant European language, culture, and systems of belief. In *Genocidal Love,* the section recounting Myrtle's three years at the school and the horrific abuse she suffered there is exceptionally short, sixteen pages. It is one of the most harrowing descriptions of the abuses suffered by inmates of the schools that I have ever read. Take care of yourselves as you read this section and remember to admire the strength of the story-sharer, Bevann Fox. The three years of hell described here with such brevity and force affected Myrtle for her entire life. This book is about that life journey.

This âcimisowin is one of the most singular ruminations on life after residential schooling that I have come across. I was struck by two things. First, I have never read such a careful parsing of the ways in which childhood abuses suffered at the schools affect adult romantic relationships. Second is the detailed description of the claims processes *pre-TRC*, including the Independent Assessment Process (IAP). Many survivors of residential schools sought justice and compensation individually through the legal system. Here, Myrtle describes the re-traumatizing process of making her first claim against the government and Church, and her devastation when the government denied the accusations. Also described in the novel is the Alternative Dispute Resolution process, which was part of the 2003 National Resolution Framework. This was followed by a large class action suit resulting in the Indian Residential School Settlement Agreement (2006). This agreement provided a Common Experience Payment for eligible former students of residential schools. It also created an Independent Assessment Process for those who suffered severe physical and/or sexual abuse. *Genocidal Love* takes readers through these labyrinthian processes and their effects on the main character, Myrtle, who repeatedly finds herself in the terrible position of having to re-narrate the abuses that put her on a life-long journey of healing. The IAP remains an under-discussed part of the settlement process with survivors, which is another reason why this novel is so important to read and teach.

A generous kēhtē-aya (old one; Elder) shared with me the Cree view of the awāsis (bright spirit; child). She drew a circle representing the awāsis. She drew another circle around the awāsis, representing a surrounding kinship system of love and care, including parents, grandparents, siblings, and extended family members. When the government removed children from the centre of the family circle and put them in the boxed residential school system, they disconnected the child from their language, culture, land, family, and identity. They broke the circle of relations and therefore of being. The broken circle and its legacies are with us to this day. This book is deeply concerned with healing from barbarous governmental systems of control, containment, and, ultimately, genocide. Many authors of residential school literature have used writing as one form of therapy on their healing journeys. So too does Bevann Fox. This book has much to teach us about strength, resistance, recovery, and reconnection. The stories of survivors of residential schooling are offerings that we need to value, respect, and share with others. We need to honour Bevann Fox for sharing her âcimisowin with us. Kinanâskomitin.

—Michelle Coupal, PhD; Canada Research Chair in Truth, Reconciliation, and Indigenous Literatures; Associate Professor, Department of English, University of Regina

ACKNOWLEDGEMENTS

This research was undertaken, in part, thanks to funding from the Canada Research Chairs Program and the Social Sciences and Humanities Research Council of Canada. I thank my research assistant, Jocelyne Paulhus, for crafting the study questions.

WORKS CITED

Alexie, Robert Arthur. *Porcupines and China Dolls*. Stoddart, 2002.

———. "Robert Arthur-Alexie—An Author in Waiting." *Indian Country Today*, 31 July 2002, pp. D1+.

Campbell, Maria. *Halfbreed*. U of Nebraska Press, 1973.

Cheechoo, Shirley. *Path with No Moccasins*. Talent Group, 1993.

Eigenbrod, Renate. "'For the child taken, for the parent left behind': Residential School Narratives as Acts of 'Survivance.'" *English Studies in Canada*, vol. 38, no. 3–4, 2012, pp. 277–297.

French, Alice. *My Name Is Masak*. Peguis, 1977.

Highway, Tomson. *Kiss of the Fur Queen*. Doubleday, 1998.

Joe, Rita. *Song of Rita Joe: Autobiography of a Mi'kmaq Poet*. U of Nebraska P, 1996.

Johnston, Basil H. *Indian School Days*. U of Oklahoma Press, 1988.

Kenny, George. *Gaawiin Mawisiiwag Anishinaabeg Indians Don't Cry*. 1977. Translated by Patricia M. Ningewance, edited by Renate Eigenbrod, U of Manitoba Press, 2014.

Manuel, Vera. *Honouring the Strength of Indian Women: Plays, Stories, Poetry*. Edited by Michelle Coupal, Deanna Reder, Joanne Arnott, Emalene A Manuel, U of Manitoba Press, 2019.

McKegney, Sam. *Magic Weapons: Aboriginal Writers Remaking Community after Residential School*. Foreword by Basil H. Johnston, U of Manitoba Press, 2007.

Sterling, Shirley. *My Name Is Seepeetza*. Groundwood Books/House of Anansi Press, 1992.

Willis, Jane. *Geniesh: An Indian Girlhood*. New Press, 1973.

PREFACE

Genocidal Love is a fictionalized telling of my own story. I was a little girl, a lot like young Myrtle, growing up on the reserve and then, later, experiencing the horrors of residential school. I was also a young woman acting out my school trauma by engaging in self-harm and in toxic relationships with unsuitable men. And today, like Myrtle, I'm a mature woman, with a successful career, a loving family, and a re-engagement with my traditional culture.

The character of Myrtle is also bigger, though, than my own personal story. She represents thousands of other little First Nations girls who experienced residential school, or who were otherwise separated from their parents or grandparents and who suffered abuse. Myrtle also represents thousands of other First Nations women who stumbled from relationship to genocidal relationship, abandoned their children out of a genocidal love for alcohol and partying and the dark allure of self-destruction.

At her best, Myrtle represents all that Indigenous women of my generation are today, or all that they could be—women who made their way back; strong, independent First Nations women who still feel crazy sometimes and can't forgive themselves for certain things they've done in their past, but who still wake up every morning and face their day with strength and resilience and faith in their beauty as human beings.

Genocidal Love—which was called *Abstract Love* when I first self-published it almost a decade ago—is largely a retelling of my own story, but back when I first wrote it, I felt I had no choice but to fictionalize it. As early as 1994, I'd been writing about my experience of residential school as I went through counselling, therapy, and ceremonies to help me heal the abuse I endured as a child. I reviewed my journals, diaries, and notes from childhood to present. I documented the claim process against the Church and government and formatted that into a memoir. I started to create a story of truth for my children and grandchildren so they could break this cycle of genocidal effects should they go through any remnants of them, so they could live their precious, beautiful lives to their fullest.

Then, in 2005, after a lengthy, intrusive experience like my hero Myrtle experiences in this book, I, like many other survivors, accepted a cash settlement from the federal government for my traumatic residential school experience. I almost immediately regretted it. I had money, but almost no sense of justice being done. And I, like all other the survivors who accepted settlements, gave up the right to sue the government for any future compensation.

I also felt unable to tell my story, even though I badly wanted to. My lawyer certainly advised me back then not to write this as a non-fiction memoir. But I refused to be silent. If a non-fiction memoir was out of the question, I would turn my life into fiction and write a novel.

So, I began *Abstract Love,* with the help of an amazing editing team, Danyta Kennedy and Christine Harrop. It took long days over two months to change my memoir to fiction. Days of back and forth phone calls, texting, and emails between us three. Days of crying, grief, and shock as I relived the experiences, as I spoke details of the horrific abuse. Both of them cried with me.

My co-editors didn't go to residential school like I did, but people close to them did. So, of course, they were triggered and suffered along with me when we were working on the original manuscript. But they did not let me quit when I felt like giving up. We had to keep going.

Finally, the manuscript was printed. And on September 15, 2011, my book was launched. I then started to travel with it and promote it and do public readings. By so doing, *Abstract Love* found its first audience, primarily an Indigenous one here in Saskatchewan, and most notably—and most pleasingly—it was a hit among Indigenous youth.

Although *Abstract Love* received that initial warm reaction, love even, I knew it could be made even better with more editorial help and, possibly, find a wider national audience if

I brought it to an established publisher. That brought me to University of Regina Press and a collaboration with my new editors, first Jorie Halcro and then, later on, Sarah Harvey.

Retitled *Genocidal Love,* it covers the same ground as *Abstract Love* but tells my character Myrtle's story with more power than before. Even if you already read *Abstract Love,* I recommend reading this version right through to the end. I think you'll appreciate the difference.

I have to say, though, that despite the good feelings I have about *Genocidal Love* today, I'm still forced to live with the fact that the effects of genocide will never be over, that the trauma I experienced will never completely go away. I wrote earlier that I created this story of truth for my children and grandchildren in the hope that they could break the cycle of genocidal effects and live their precious, beautiful lives to the fullest. You will see a symbol of this hope in the final chapter, "We Are Royalty Too." Like my son, Myrtle's son gives Prince Charles of England a tour of his high school and attends a basketball game with him. Like my grandsons, Myrtle's eldest grandson dances for the great-great-great-grandson of the queen who signed the Treaties with my ancestors; Myrtle's youngest grandson, at twelve years old, delivers a speech about the Treaties before the queen's representative. The ending of *Genocidal Love* offers hope that, with the new generation, this story can be freed from its fictional self.

Today I am just me, a normal person living a successful, happy, healthy life, although with the disruption of genocidal effects here and there. I will live with them forever. Anxiety is everywhere in my body as I type this preface. I feel anger too. It's possible to feel every emotion. But I will work through all this and continue. I hope you understand and can find some compassion and awareness of the reality in Canada when it comes to the lasting and multi-generational effects of residential school trauma. You may never know what it is like to live with genocidal effects, but *Genocidal Love* will take you there.

There are many of us Myrtles, both female and male, out there. I know there are. Perhaps justice will come out of the publication of this new and improved version of my original novel. I can only pray for that.

Nowadays, freedom for me is simply enjoying my morning coffee on the back deck when the weather is fine, grateful that I can make delicious Sunday dinners for my beautiful children and grandchildren. Sometimes, though, my mind wanders as I sip my coffee, and I think about all the damage and trauma inflicted on Indigenous people like me over the last few hundred years ... and then these lines from my novel come to me:

> Myrtle thought of Yellow Dog Breast. "Where are you? Did you see this coming?" she said. "You saw this for the future, but the leaders didn't listen. They signed the Treaties, the Treaties were to last for as long as the sun shines, the grass grows and the rivers flow."

—Bevann Fox, Regina, September 2020

GENOCIDAL LOVE

PROLOGUE

Once upon a time there was a beautiful land with millions of beautiful Red People who lived a traditional peaceful life in balance with the nature of Mother Earth. One day a wicked queen from another world came to visit. She was amazed with the beautiful land and the beautiful Red People. "My, my, what do we have here?" she said in a cackling, shrill voice. She turned to her men in silver shining armour. "Get ready for battle; we will take over this land and all the Red People!"

The queen turned to her representative, a short, fat, balding man. "Go and represent me and meet with the Red People. Fool them with a piece of paper called a Treaty. We will fill it with promises. They cannot read, speak, or write English anyway. Invite the Red Leaders to sign this Treaty paper with any kind of mark because they can't write. That piece of paper with their mark will give me control of all the lands, and I promise to take care of the Red People as my own little red children. I will be their mother dearest, and I am the richest, fairest one in all the lands! I will take care of the red children forever and ever!" The wicked queen laughed and laughed.

The Treaty was written with promises. It was talked about between the Red People and the queen's men. The queen promised in the Treaty that if the Red People surrendered the land, they would get gun powder, a brick school, health and wellness, reservations to live on and five dollars each year. This Treaty was to last forever, as long as the sun shines, the grass grows, and the rivers flow. It would never be broken.

Yellow Dog Breast came to the signing of the Treaty in the beautiful valley. He was very angry as he walked forward to the front line. Everyone stopped to look at him. Yellow Dog Breast was strikingly beautiful. He stood tall as he held his robe around him. Finally, he threw off his robe and stood completely naked! Yellow Dog Breast gave out a cry to the heavens. He threw up his arms and jumped in the air and then fell to his knees. He leaned forward and kissed the ground and said, "*This is my land!*"

The queen laughed and laughed as her representative told the story about Yellow Dog Breast. Yellow Dog Breast may have stopped the signing of the Treaty briefly, but his own Red People did not listen. As the queen sang "this land is my land, forever and ever," all her horses and men danced along beside her and she lived happily ever after.

PART ONE

Nōhkom and Nimosōm

LIFE WAS GOOD

I GREW UP ON THE RESERVE JUST SOUTH OF A BIG city. The reserve was covered with lots of trees and hills. My grandparents were called Nōhkom and Nimosōm. They took care of ten children: me and my younger brother and sister, and seven cousins. My mother was there too, but sometimes she left the house and reservation for a while to work at different jobs in the city, cleaning or cooking, but never for a long time. The longest she left us was a year. When she was home, she worked hard to take care of all of us—washing clothes by hand and scrubbing the walls and floors.

Once a week I had a bath in a big round silver tub in the same water everyone else used. I hated bathing in the dirty water, particularly because the younger kids often peed in it, so I would hurry to be the first one in the tub. In winter my grandparents chopped ice from the dam nearby and gathered snow to melt on the stove. The water was used for drinking, cooking, and washing. "It has to be clean," Nimosōm said. "Be careful not to gather dirty snow."

One day, Nimosōm pulled us in a sleigh and I started to cry as I stared at his back. I had suddenly realized that my grandfather was not so healthy. His eyesight was weak, and he was getting old. I thought he was going to die. I wanted Nimosōm to live forever. Who else would take care of us? Later that night I asked him not to die. Nimosōm talked with me about death, but I still could not bear the thought of losing him.

Nōhkom made fresh bannock every day and we ate deer, rabbit, duck, and prairie chickens. Sometimes Nimosōm cut fence pickets and sold them to nearby farmers so we could buy food. The kids helped Nimosōm carry the trees from the bush. It was fun. Mostly we loved getting praise for the work we did. We wanted to show Nimosōm and Nōhkom how strong we were, so we competed against one another. There was complaining and arguing over who pushed who into the pinch bushes, which had thorns that hurt and sometimes stayed stuck in the skin.

We attended lodge ceremonies, although I never participated. "A long time ago we weren't allowed to practise the ceremonies," Nimosōm told us. "The Rain Dance was a ceremony that was done every year. The government stopped the Indian people from practising the traditions passed on from my grandfathers. They have control over everything we do." Nimosōm talked about the Ghost Dance, the Shake Tent, the piercing and pulling of skin that is a significant sacred sacrifice at the Rain Dance. I could not believe all that happened in the different ceremonies he described. He said, "If you believe...you could move a mountain," and, "You do not talk about what happens in the ceremonies, because it is very sacred. The white men come around here being nosy with their cameras. The white ones, they want to look at everything under a microscope and they have to explain everything, make it like a test in science and sell it to make money."

I said, "Nimosōm, I am too scared to go to ceremony, and I won't tell anyone about them!"

Nimosōm smiled. "Why are you afraid? Don't be afraid. You must pray every day, sometimes do a fast and give up something—go without food and water for one day." Nimosōm's words rang in my ears. "You put the Creator first, then yourself. You must believe in yourself!" When Nimosōm started his four-day fast, he sometimes let me fast for a day or half a day. At the end of the day he prayed and gave me the blessed rainwater to drink. He prayed over the soup and bannock. He said, "Sometimes we take the simple things in life for granted."

As I swallowed the fresh, cool rainwater, I could feel it going down my throat. How I loved and appreciated that drink! And I thanked the Creator. The soup and bannock was the most delicious meal ever! I thanked the Creator... for *life*!

I attended powwows too. My dance outfits were later passed on to the younger children. The powwows were so much fun! Nimosōm set up camp and people from far away came to visit. At powwows there was so much laughter and excitement in the air. Every day there was something to do and people to see. Nimosōm said, "A long time ago, before the powwow became competitive and commercialized, the sweetgrass smudge scent carried for miles and miles." As he spoke, I closed my eyes and smelled the sweetgrass scent far from the powwow grounds. I didn't know yet what *commercialized* meant.

Often, people who came to the powwows stayed on at my family's home. My grandparents gave the visitors gifts of fabrics, blankets, or beaded items. Visitors were treated like kings and queens in our home. The children were to wait on them, serve them meals, and treat them with respect. We were never to stare at people because it was rude. I liked to stare at people, and often Nōhkom scolded me and said in Cree to stop staring, "Ēkawiya pakisapi."

Nimosōm and Nōhkom's home was warm and comfortable. It smelled nice, like apples and sage. Nimosōm helped people who came to see him from near and far. He was a Medicine Man. I could hear the prayers, the songs, the special whistle blowing, and the rattle shaking.

Nimosōm once told me about a woman with a sickness called cancer. Cancer ate the insides and it was very painful and those who had the sickness would often die. I went with Nimosōm to pick roots from the ground in the bush. He crushed the roots and made medicines to drink and smudge. I watched him make colours from the ground. The colours he used for special things like paint for the teepee. The teepee was put up every spring and used for ceremonies and feasts. It stood tall and beautiful. The designs painted on the teepee had significant meaning. The thunderbird, for example, is a name in our family. Many of us are named after the thunderbird. Also, painted circles signify life cycles, the seasons, and the directions.

THE QUEEN BEE

During my early childhood, I enjoyed the feeling of security that was the heritage of my family. A strong, invisible web, rich in life, colour, and emotion. I was accepted by my grandparents and, like the other children and grandchildren, I had a nickname. I always knew when my grandparents were talking about me because they communicated in Cree. Both my grandparents also spoke Saulteaux, and Nōhkom spoke Michif and French. I learned to understand Cree but when I tried to speak it, only fragmented sentences mixed with English came out. My grandparents often became upset with me when I couldn't answer them in Cree.

Aunt Eve, like my mother, was a beautiful woman. My uncle called me "Li'l Eve" because he said I looked like my aunt. I imagined that Aunt Eve was my real mother and I felt proud. Sometimes he called me "Betty." Betty lived across the road. This made me feel even more proud! He was teasing me but I accepted it like a compliment because to me, Eve and Betty were the most beautiful women on the reserve besides my momma. Sometimes I really did wonder if Betty was my real mother, because I had the same fair skin and freckles that both Betty and Aunt Eve had. When I saw them, I would stare and look for a sign that one of them was my mom. I waited for one of them to say, "I am your mother, you are my daughter." When my mother was away I was so lonesome. When she was home, my momma fixed her hair, wore lovely clothes, and smelled nice all the time. So, when she was away, Betty and Aunt Eve would be around and I would pretend they were my moms.

As a child, I was always excited to go to the big city. People with blond hair and blue eyes fascinated me. I would stare at them until Nōhkom gave me a little pinch and said, "Ēkawiya pakisapi!" *Don't stare!* But I stared anyway and asked many questions because I was curious.

One of the places they shopped at in the city was Simpsons-Sears. When I was about four years old, I was in the elevator with my grandparents and mother. On that particular day, I didn't like my mother's bossiness; she grabbed my arm so roughly that it hurt. *She's mean,* I thought. *She is not my mother!* I wanted to run freely in the department store and hide in the hanging clothes. That was fun! The clothes were so new and I liked the way they smelled, but my mother wouldn't let me go. Other people were in the elevator with us when I said, "Bitch."

"Pōyo," Nōhkom said. *Quit.*

I repeated it louder and louder. "Bitch, bitch, bitch!" Then I said, "Fuckin' bitch," calmly at first. The first time I heard the words *fuckin' bitch* was when I saw a man hit a woman as they walked down the street. I had felt scared because I knew those were bad words. My mother kept pinching me but I kept repeating the words in hope of embarrassing her. After the elevator incident, Nimosōm and Nōhkom were very upset with me. They told me that there would be no more city visits for me because of my behaviour; I would have to stay at home from now on. They kept their word, and the next time they left for the city I ran after the car, screaming in the dust and throwing myself to the ground crying. Nimosōm and Nōhkom just kept on driving down the road.

That was a long day. My siblings and cousins and I watched and waited as cars sped by, hoping each one was Nimosōm and Nōhkom. We made up songs and played a guessing game as we waited. Finally, we spotted our grandparents driving up the road toward the house. We went crazy with happiness, screaming, laughing, and hugging each other! Everyone was hungry because there was no food in the house.

Later that night a fancy meal was prepared. Potatoes, sausages, and spareribs were boiled in the same pot, tomatoes were sliced on to a plate, cream-style corn was put in a bowl, and sliced white bread was set on the table. The children each got a bag of chips, a bottle of warm Coke, and a chocolate bar to have after supper. Our grandparents loved to see us so happy.

Nimosōm prayed and blessed the food with sweetgrass smudge. A special plate for an offering was prepared and prayed for and then placed outside in a clean area by a tree, where no dogs could get at it. The offering was to feed the spirits—my grandparents' loved ones who had died—so they too could eat in the spirit world. The respect for this was so great that we all waited quietly for Nimosōm to finish praying even though our mouths watered and our stomachs growled with hunger. Finally, the prayer was finished and Nimosōm said, "Ahum mīcisok!" *Everybody eats!*

Nōhkom wore rouge and lipstick for special days. She was so pretty. Sometimes she let me put some on. Nōhkom's broaches, earrings, rings, and scarves were very beautiful. I loved the way Nōhkom smelled of perfume and Doublemint gum. She always had gum to give to me. When we were alone, Nōhkom let me look at her jewelry and play with it for a while. The pieces were mostly there to admire. Nōhkom wore different floral dresses for different occasions, and her thick beige stockings were held up above each knee with an elastic band.

Nōhkom often told me that I talked too much, but she would comfort me by rubbing my head and running her fingers through my long hair. I especially liked touching Nōhkom's arm to feel her skin. It felt so loose, flabby, and soft. I would ask Nōhkom if I could touch her flabby soft arm while she told stories about her younger days and sang songs in Cree. I remember her singing, *Edmonton* "ē-itoh- tē- yān," *automobile* "ē- pōsi- yān. Mōniyaskwēw ē-itēy-mi-soyān. ē-cika ōma ē-otihko miya..." *Edmonton driving in an automobile. Acting like a white woman feeling good about it, but I had lice in my hair...* The way she sang that song was so funny. Her laughter as we joined in. It was hilarious!

Nōhkom would buy tubes of baloney and cut the slices thick, just the way I liked them. I loved baloney and ketchup. I dipped the baloney into the ketchup and looked at Nōhkom. Once again, I noticed the skin above her elbows, hanging so loose, her hands and fingers bent up as she used both hands to lift her rolled cigarette to her mouth. But even with her bent and twisted fingers, Nōhkom cut the most perfect baloney slices and I thought the slices were beautiful because Nōhkom cut them, and Nōhkom was beautiful.

Nimosōm washed my hair once a week with a special shampoo called White Rain. This was my favourite shampoo, and I loved the scent. He used fresh rainwater from the barrel to rinse my hair and then he brushed out all the knots and tangles. "Respect your hair, for it is a part of you. Don't leave it lying around, it is sacred. Don't cut your hair," he said.

Every spring Nimosōm washed my hair in boiled sweetgrass water, when the grass was new, having just sprung from the earth. Nimosōm said my hair would grow like the grass grows. And it did grow very fast! Other times he washed my hair in cold black tea that had sat for days. All of this helped my hair to stay healthy and strong and it grew very long. Nimosōm kept loose strands of my hair in a bag and when the bag was full we burned it.

When it rained, Nimosōm prepared our home for prayer and smudged each room. Then he smudged the children with sweetgrass smudge. It was so comforting. The rumbling cracks of thunder came, and the rain showers followed. We felt safe in our grandparents' home as we listened to the thunder move across the sky. Our eyes grew huge at the sound of the thunder and we giggled together. Nimosōm talked about the thunderbird and how the bird's spirit protected us. I had a picture in my mind of huge, beautiful thunderbirds watching over our home. Sometimes, when the lightning stopped, Nimosōm let us run out in the rain and shampoo our hair with the raindrops. We laughed and ran in the rain, having so much fun!

Nimosōm loved listening to my stories. He would make tea and put sugar and evaporated milk into my cup before settling at the table to talk. Sometimes we argued over something but Nimosōm would smile and say, "Okay, Mōniyāskwēsis *[Little White Girl]*, you win." He challenged me on everything, and sometimes I found it difficult to stay in an argument. But it was fun to talk and talk and to say what was on my mind.

The Jehovah's Witnesses and Mormon missionaries came around to visit, handing out pamphlets and reading materials. Nimosōm went outside to meet them and talked for a very long time, asking questions about their beliefs and their churches. He never sent them away. Sometimes I heard him arguing with the missionaries. Nimosōm believed in prayer anywhere. "Pray in your mind, talk to the Creator in your heart," he said to the missionaries. "You don't have to go to a church." Even though Nimosōm argued with the missionaries, he liked their visits and loved the debate. "A real good talking argument," Nimosōm called it. The missionaries always left frustrated with my grandfather. Yet they would come again to visit.

Every morning there was work to do and play had to wait until later in the day. Sometimes, when I was feeling lazy and did not want to work, I went outside to the outhouse and stayed in there for a long time, hoping the dishes would be done by the time I went back into the house. The toilet stunk, and I gagged as I looked through old catalogues. Toilet paper was a luxury, and it disappeared very fast so there was a box of newspaper, brown paper, and rags on the floor beside the toilet. Oh…and the flies. "Those dirty rotten bastards!" Nimosōm swore at the flies every day. They were pests and germ carriers. I took a can of Raid, which Nimosōm kept hidden, and sprayed the toilet before I entered.

At nighttime a pail called the slop pail was put by the door. I hated the job of emptying it the next morning. The mess sprayed back in my face as I gagged and complained about the other kids using the slop pail during the night. I called them cowards for being scared to go outside to the toilet at night. Sometimes going to that toilet was a nightmare but, when I was in there, I screamed for privacy because my cousins and siblings would throw stones at the toilet to disturb and startle me. I would run inside the house to tell on the others, and Nimosōm and Nōhkom would try to calm me down.

The bush was a beautiful escape. I took comic books and a catalogue and set out on my journey alone. Sometimes I brought a jar of Kool-Aid and some baloney sandwiches for a picnic. I sat in the warm sun in the old cars abandoned in the bushes, looking at every page of the clothing catalogue. I dreamed of making and wearing beautiful clothes someday. On every page I saw myself wearing the clothes, and I said out loud, "That's me, there is me and that is me again."

I loved the smell of the trees and plants in the warm sun, the sounds of the birds. I could hear the other kids looking for me and wondered, "Why can't they just leave me alone?"

I knew every trail like the back of my hand and ran through them barefoot. Sometimes I would climb a tree and watch the others looking for me, calling my name. A butterfly would flutter by and stop to sit on my fingers; it was so delicate and beautiful. I told myself not to move or even breathe. I would look at its pretty wings and smell its dusty scent. "You're a sacred butterfly." The different blended colours on the wings were so amazing and beautiful! "Fly away, pretty one." I remembered Nimosōm and Nōhkom's words: "Never hurt living things; each has its own spirit. The trees and the rocks have spirits too. Everything has a spirit!"

The children weren't allowed to break branches off trees. It was disrespectful and hurtful to the tree. It was tempting at times to break off a branch filled with berries and eat from the broken branch, but the guilt that followed was not worth it. Instead, we picked the berries off the bushes with our fingers. It was sheer laziness if we broke branches, and we really got in trouble if we did.

I would smile and ask Nimosōm, "Why are you so mean to the flies?"

"The flies will always be dirty!" Nimosōm said.

"Don't the flies have a spirit too, since they are alive?" I asked.

"I never really thought of them, but I'm sure they have a place on earth too, maybe to bug us, drive us crazy and make us grouchy!" Nimosōm laughed.

Once I set the other kids on a race to the beehive and then threw a rock from a distance. I regretted destroying the bee's home, but I did it only to get back at the other kids and to try to get them to stay away from me. They were stung many times. I smiled with sweet revenge. When I got home, however, I paid the price twice over. My grandparents were so upset and disappointed in me. I explained that I just wanted to be left alone—not bothered or followed—but the other kids wouldn't leave me alone. The troublemakers were standing there with bee stings all over their faces, arms, and legs. "Respect life in the bush because if you don't, something will come back on you, you may get hurt. That was a home you destroyed, and you caused your brothers and sisters pain," my grandparents said.

For the next few days I waited to be punished. I was so afraid and felt so sorry for the bees. Where would they live? It took me a long time to realize that my punishment was to understand how bad it was that I had destroyed the bees' home.

NO TEARS

MY MOTHER TOLD US THAT WE CAME FROM A huge family on Nōhkom's side and were related to many families in the Treaty Territory; on Nimosōm's side we were related to many more families. She told us all the names of our relatives and explained the importance of family. "When you meet people," she explained, "let them know who you are and also your grandparents' names because your name tells a story of your kinship and family history. It is to keep the respect of kinship. It is so important to know who we are. It is an unwritten law."

Old Chichi was my grandmother's uncle. He was blind. We children were always well behaved and quiet when he came from the neighbouring rez to visit our grandparents. Old Chichi walked everywhere, visiting people. He sawed piles and piles of wood for our family. We were scared of him because it was as if he could see right through us. Nōhkom said that old man Chichi knew when we were misbehaving, and he might hit us with his cane. I always felt that Chichi saw us even if we stood far away and tried not to stare. When I served him tea at Nōhkom's order, I would start to shake when I went near him.

Sometimes I walked and ran barefoot through the bush, pretending to be blind like Old Chichi, and I walked through the paths in the bush, my eyes closed, trying to imagine what it felt like to have super powers like Chichi. But the others told our grandparents that I was making fun of Old Chichi, which I would never do.

There was another old man, a relative of Nimosōm's, who came to visit from the south. Uncle Roderick, my mother's older brother and a great storyteller, told me that this man wore heavy clothes and had a wallet full of bills in his pants' pocket and change in another pocket and that he understood and spoke German very well. This old man always carried a jar of tea on his journeys.

Kōhkom Sky lived close to us. She was very old. I would see her coming to visit and wait anxiously for her arrival. Nōhkom sent the children outside to play, but I wanted to stay and listen. The bannock and tea was ready and I wanted to be the one to serve Kōhkom Sky. I was happy when Nōhkom said I could stay, and I sat down to listen and watch. Often Kōhkom Sky and Nimosōm exchanged medicines. They talked about me and teasingly said that I was a nosy little white girl because I wanted to know everything. They called me "Mōniyāskwēsis" *(Little White Girl)*, but they were smiling when they said it. All the old people on the rez called me Mōniyāskwēsis.

Nimosōm and Nōhkom would tell Kōhkom Sky about my latest "incidents" and Kōhkom Sky would laugh. I loved the sound of her laughter and loved the scent of her—she smelled of sage. Kōhkom Sky was a comfort, and I felt nurtured by her just being there. I knew I stared at Kōhkom Sky, but that was because I was amazed and mesmerized by her. I loved the scarves that were tied under her chin and I loved the coloured-print dresses she wore. I knew her walk and could imitate it. I studied her hands, the way she ate and drank her tea. I loved the sound of her voice. Kōhkom Sky did not speak English, only Cree.

Once, I got very sick, and my mother said that my illness was due to my heart and kidneys, and that my blood was too thin. I was a pale, sickly looking child. I slept for days, and I thought I might be dying.

Kōhkom Sky came to the house to see me. I knew she was in my room because I could smell her sage scent. She and Nimosōm prayed and burned a mixed-root smudge. Kōhkom Sky gave me something to drink while Nimosōm sang a song with his rattle and blew a whistle on me. I felt safe, happy, and warm, and I recovered and was happy to play outside once again and run through the bushes.

"Nimosōm," I said, "when you die can you come visit me and let me know if you are in that special place called home? But why do you call it home when your home is here?"

"Mōniyāskwēsis, you will be scared, and you will pee your pants!" Nimosōm laughed.

"No, I won't. Please, Nimosōm. You have to come visit me."

"Believe in the Creator, the Creator is greater than all of us," Nimosōm said as he began to sing at the table, humming one of those special songs he sung with the hand drum or the rattle. I waited until he was done.

"Can I talk now, Nimosōm?"

"What now, Ceecee?" Nimosōm asked, smiling in the other direction. Nimosōm had three names for me: Chee, Ceecee, and Mōniyāskwēsis.

"Why don't you come visit me in a dream?" I was breathless with excitement at coming up with such a great idea.

After pausing for a long time, he answered. "All right, I'll visit you in the dream, Ceecee, but only if you promise to put a box of Lucky Elephant popcorn in the coffin." The pink popcorn in a box tasted like sweet candy and it was Nimosōm's favourite. My mouth watered at the thought of eating that sweet popcorn.

Christmas and New Year's holidays were huge celebrations in my community. Every household got in the Christmas spirit! We wore our best clothes and people came to eat with our family. It was a tradition that the big meal began at midnight on Christmas Eve. At that time, presents from Santa were opened and they usually were the same for all the children; no one received anything different. One Christmas, the girls all got dolls of different colours and the boys got the same car or truck. Another Christmas we received toy accordions, and the following year it was silver airplanes with a flashing red light. I loved the way the toys smelled of plastic. Oh, and those coloured, curly Christmas candies! Real Christmas candies. On Christmas day kids walked from house to house, eating. Some homes had little or nothing to eat, but they still gave something to those who came by. The candies and desserts were so delicious. At each home we were greeted with kisses.

Sometimes I had to stay in the house and work during the holiday season. I washed dishes all day and set the table for the next visitors. And I waited for Kōhkom Sky. My grandparents' home was decorated with Christmas ornaments and all their many Christmas cards hung in a row from a string stretched across the wall. The house smelled like Christmas oranges, Jell-O, and Christmas candies. Everything was Christmas! It was the spirit of family. Nōhkom and I spent hours in the store searching for pretty fabrics that looked rich and delicate. Nōhkom gave the cloth, along with beautiful ribbon, as gifts to visitors.

New Year was the same tradition all over again, every year. Everybody greeted each other with kisses. So many kisses and so much to eat! It was exciting!

All year round the children looked at pictures in the Sears catalogue. Nōhkom called the catalogue the "wish book." When the other children ripped a page out while arguing, "Mine," and "No, that's me and that's mine," it made me mad.

Surely it drove Nōhkom insane, although she didn't show it. That wish book eventually ended up in the stinky toilet.

My mom drove me around to trade my comic books with other kids on the rez. I was a comic collector and kept my comic books in good shape. My favourite was *Betty and Veronica*. I loved the way they dressed. Betty had yellow hair; she was what I pictured women looked like in the outside world. I didn't like to trade my comics for used ones because I liked my comics and books new. But I wanted to read, so I reluctantly traded. My mother told me to share my comic books so someone else could read them too.

My mother and grandparents took the children along with them to local garbage dumps on the outskirts of small towns. I did not like the trips to the dumps and quickly became irritated by all the screaming and noise from my siblings and cousins. It made me feel crazy! But I went along for the ride, hoping for a treat of candy, chips, or ice cream. I developed a rash if I touched any of the stuff in the dump. Nimosōm went through things in the dump while Nōhkom sat in the car, puffing big clouds of smoke while using both hands to hold her rolled cigarette and watching the kids run around out of control. Nimosōm found things like pieces of scrap metal and copper, which he later sold in the big city for money to buy food and clothes for our family. He made deals with the store people wherever he went, always asking to speak with the owner or manager of the store.

When my mom was just learning how to drive a car, I was in the back seat and opened the door and tried to close it while the car was moving. I was trying to copy the adults I had seen doing that. But when the wind caught the door, I was pulled out of the vehicle and thrown across the road. I could hear Nōhkom screaming at my mother to stop. The wind was knocked out of me and I struggled to catch my breath. When I did, I screamed hysterically. I was stunned and scared but wasn't hurt. My mother got a scolding from Nōhkom and I felt sad about that. She hadn't done anything wrong.

It was always a long drive to the city because my mother pulled over to side of the highway whenever she met an oncoming car. On one of the drives, my cousin Pauline, who was from the city, asked, "What is the matter with Aunty?"

"She is learning how to drive," I whispered.

I often got carsick, my face turning white as I gagged. Nōhkom would scream, talking hysterically in Cree, and my mother, overwhelmed and in a panic, stopped the car on the side of the road and pulled me out so that I could vomit. Sometimes other kids in the car annoyed me and smelling their breath made me want to vomit. I ignored them until I couldn't take it anymore and screamed at them for not cleaning their mouths properly.

If the children fought or argued in the car, my mother whipped them good with a twig she had picked up on the side of the road and kept under the front seat of the car. I was often the one getting hit on the leg with that twig.

On one trip I "cried" all the way to town and all the way back to the rez. I was determined to show my grandparents and my mother that the car rides really hurt me. But they paid no attention to me. Instead, they told the story to everyone on the reserve who came to visit. Kōhkom Sky came over and they all laughed at the story. "Wah-wah-hiy!" *Holy smokes!* Kōhkom Sky said. Uncle Roderick told the story even though he wasn't there. I sure felt silly about "crying" all the way to town and back. "It was twenty-eight miles of crying," they said, "and we wondered how her eyes got red with no tears." They told that story forever. "Remember the day Myrtle cried all the way to town and back with no tears?"

PREGNANT MEANS KISSING

Sometimes my mother took us to our aunt's home in the big city. I loved going there because they had a bathroom with a toilet that flushed, and—oh my gosh!—a phone and nice furniture. It was exciting!

My cousin Pauline and I were very close. Pauline knew all the games to play and appeared to be more mature than me. Pauline had great plans to share with me. She knew things the other kids did not and was a leader of all the kids when we went to the city. Pauline was tough and could fight or talk herself out of any situation. She talked and laughed loudly. Pauline and I were at a movie once and there were kissing parts. Pauline turned to me and whispered, "Do you feel funny when you see this?"

"No," I said.

"I do, it makes me feel like I need to pee!" Pauline whispered. We laughed, but I wondered why Pauline felt this way.

Even so, I laughed, pretending I understood. Also, her shrill, shrieking laugh was so funny it made me laugh even harder!

The sliding hill in the coulee on the rez was a fun place to be in the winter. The kids used car hoods and cardboard to slide down the hill because there were no toboggans or sleighs. Neighbours would join in, and sometimes someone got hurt. Shawna and the twins from down the road also played with us.

Shawna was my good friend, almost like a sister. It felt like they were family because they lived so close and we spent a lot of time together. Shawna worked hard at home, helping her Nōhkom and taking care of her little brothers. I was afraid of Shawna's Nōhkom, who would yell for her so loudly that you could hear her from far away. Shawna would have to leave and go home. Her Nōhkom was protective of them. They didn't have to go away to school at all because Shawna's Nōhkom was able to keep them at home.

Across the field were my friends Cowboy and Gina. I stole rolled cigarettes from Nōhkom, and the girls and I smoked them. My first time smoking was in the stinky toilet. Sometimes we smoked behind the house by the toilet. I coughed, almost choking on the smoke. Gina looked so grown up smoking the rolled cigarette. She showed me how to smoke, but I could not inhale; the smoke burned my lungs. We all laughed and laughed, having so much fun together and never arguing or fighting. The girls didn't like being bothered by the younger kids or boys. Cowboy was the strong one; she could rough handle anyone, and her loud, tough voice was enough to scare the boys away. She tuned them up good! "*Get the hell out of here!*" Cowboy would yell at the boys, who took off running scared. Cowboy's yell would even scare me, but the girls felt protected by her, even though she was only a couple of years older. No one ever told on us for smoking because they were too scared of Cowboy.

In the winter, the kids hung out at snow caves and forts that they built beside the river; sometimes they built bonfires on the ice. Children from all around the area stayed outdoors all day, going home only to eat. I never felt the cold when I was with my friends on the ice. Some kids were older than me, but they were all good to each other. The only problem was that I was forced to be a goalie when they played hockey. I hated it, but the other kids really cheered me on and being a goalie was the only way I felt accepted. The agreement was that I could not play with them unless I was goalie. I got hurt many times by the puck because I was so scared of it. But if I agreed to be the goalie, the kids would let me stay later for the bonfire.

The older kids did not pick on the younger ones too much, but they liked to boss them around sometimes. The older boys gave kisses and hugs to the older girls but when a young boy tried to kiss me I became upset and hit him very hard.

"Get away from me!" I yelled.

This boy had snot dripping from his nose from the cold. Nimosōm came to the top of the hill and yelled for me to come home. "*Come home now, Chee!*" I was so embarrassed.

I didn't want Nimosōm calling me by my nicknames anymore. I ran home so fast and was so angry with Nimosōm that I would not talk to him.

Grandparents on the rez never allowed the children out when it was night time. As soon as it got dark we were all called inside, and the doors were locked and the window blinds closed. That was an unwritten law. Nimosōm always reminded the kids about this, that the night should be respected and it was a time for rest. This law brought social order in our home and kept us safely away from the night. I knew this was really why Nimosōm had called me to come inside. But I was mad and went right to bed and complained to Nōhkom. Nōhkom told me to stay away from boys.

"Some dirty," Nōhkom said. "He want to poke you they make fun..." she explained in her broken English. Then she talked in Cree.

I listened then said, "Nōhkom, this boy tried to kiss me and he had bubbles of snot hanging out of his nose to his lips. Is that dirty, Nōhkom?"

"Wah-wah-hiy! Wīni-takikom." *Snotty nose.* "Why he no clean? Awīna awa?" *Who is this?* Nōhkom laughed. I didn't tell her the boy's name. I pretended to be asleep.

On the reserve, Kaya was a cousin I looked up to. She was my idol, and I copied everything about her. Kaya was strong and protected me when I was picked on. We laughed all the time. Kaya would tell me stories.

"What does pregnant mean?" I asked Kaya one day.

"Do you really want to know?" Kaya asked quietly, looking very secretive. I was very curious now, so I leaned closer and Kaya whispered in my ear, "It means you want to be kissed by a boy!" I was so startled, but Kaya started to giggle.

"*No, I don't!*" I yelled.

"So you want to be pregnant!" Kaya exclaimed as she tickled me.

"*Nooooo,*" I screamed with laughter.

Kaya knew all the answers. She was so smart! We were always in trouble for laughing so much, but we still laughed silently through our noses when we got scolded for being too loud.

Spring marked the beginning of life—the renewal of the earth, trees, and grass. Nimosōm put up the teepee with the special drawings and a feast was prepared. It was a busy time. The old ones came to share their prayers. Yes, the beginning of spring was a very special day! I loved it.

The ceremonies were rooted in the past, but I understood their complexity, their hidden meanings. The feasts were very special and the children behaved during this time. It was exciting as the preparations began. The Rain Dance was one of the lodge ceremonies. The children did their best to make things easier for their grandparents. They didn't argue with one another and listened intently for instructions. They prepared and got ready for the ceremony long before the day came. The grownups committed to this practice by making a sacrifice—no liquids at all for four days before the ceremony—and the respect and peace in the home during this time was so peaceful, warm, and beautiful.

But there were also days when we had little or no food to eat and we were all very hungry. Sometimes only bannock was in the cupboard and tea, lots of tea. When the farmers didn't want to buy Nimosōm's pickets, on the way home he would become very quiet. The seven children decided to surprise Nimosōm by getting food so Nimosōm wouldn't have to worry about us being hungry. We thought Nimosōm would be proud when we brought home a rabbit to eat. I knew where the snares were because I went with Nimosōm every day to check them, so I led the children to the snares, only to find that they were empty! Just as we were about to give up, we found the last snare, with a rabbit stuck in it. Someone grabbed the rabbit but it got loose. We chased the poor rabbit, threw rocks at it and hit it with pieces of wood but it got away! We were so disappointed. I felt sorry for the poor rabbit and somewhat happy that it got away. At the same time, I was hungry and wanted so much for Nimosōm to be proud of us and not worry. At home, we told Nimosōm the story of hunting for rabbits. He just smiled and laughed.

The next day there were lots of rabbits. The other girls and I had to help skin the rabbits and gut them. "Don't be proud, Mōniyāskwēsis," Nōhkom said to me as I gagged at the smell. Was this why they called me Little White Girl in Cree?

But that smelly rabbit sure tasted good as soup or a roast. I tried not to think of the poor rabbit being skinned and gutted. If I did, I gagged on my soup, which upset my grandparents. The others giggled as I was scolded in Cree. They bugged me so much with their teasing; they knew I was easily annoyed.

The chickens were a rotten job too. All the children gathered to see the axe cut the chickens' heads off. Then we ran away in sheer terror, screaming as the headless chickens ran after us. We ran around like crazy, just like the chickens. Afterward, the chickens were soaked in a hot tub of water and then plucked. It stunk so much that I gagged and vomited. My grandparents said I was too proud and delicate. "Mōniyāskwēsis ana," *Little White Girl, that one,* they would say. My tummy was too delicate to stomach the food, but I needed nourishment and there was no other food. At the supper table, eating the chicken was almost too much for me to take, and I gagged as I tried to put out of my mind the chicken chasing us with its head cut off.

Eating wild meat was very difficult for me because I often witnessed the slaughter of the animals. I saw animals being killed, skinned, butchered, and prepared. When I ate deer meat, I pretended to be eating an A&W hamburger from the city. Nōhkom made hamburger patties with deer meat and I made hamburger buns using bannock. I used lots of ketchup... if there was any.

Duck meat was very greasy, and I sprinkled lots of salt on it whenever I had to eat duck soup or fried duck. I thought the duck would come alive inside me and kick its way out of my stomach. If I'd had my way, all I'd eat would be ketchup or mustard with bannock or bread.

Picking berries was fun, and every year around the same time and at the same places the competition began to see who was the best, cleanest, and fastest picker. I could never keep up and I became bored and then started a fight or got someone into trouble. Someone always spilled their berries, and we would all laugh hysterically. Before the berry picking was over, I would always be the one to get sent home for causing trouble and talking back. But I was only trying to defend myself. I didn't like it when I felt picked on and everyone ganged up on me. I tried to explain this to Nōhkom, but she'd take a stick and chase me home. Although she didn't hit me, I cried all the way home. Being rejected by Nōhkom was worse than if she hit my legs with the stick.

When Nōhkom returned home from berry picking, she touched my hair and hands. Nōhkom's fingers and hands were bent and disfigured and she had a difficult time holding things, but with her bent fingers she massaged my head and arms.

During the summer, the canning preparations began. Saskatoon berries were canned in jars. I didn't understand why it was called canning when the berries were placed in glass jars, not cans. Chokecherries were crushed with a rock and my mother and Nōhkom spent hours sitting and crushing the chokecherries while telling many stories. The berries were stored away for special holidays and ceremonies. The berries tasted so yummy when fried and served on bannock.

The children were warned not to eat too many chokecherries, or they'd have problems later in the toilet.

Nimosōm taught me and the other grandchildren many things. He taught us to jig and also to hoop dance. He taught my cousins how to Grass Dance. He tried to teach me the violin, but I wasn't interested. During my lessons, I complained and cried instead of practising; I preferred to be outside playing with the others.

I loved listening to Nimosōm's songs at night. He sat at the table and quietly sang the songs passed on to him. I loved hearing him sing just before sleep overtook me. It was soothing and comforting. The following morning, I shared my dreams with Nimosōm and he interpreted them for me. He honoured my dreams.

PART TWO

Learn the Good and Leave the Bad

MEET THE QUEEN

WHEN I WAS SEVEN NIMOSŌM AND NŌHKOM decided to send me and my younger siblings Kenny and Karen to school, a boarding school. We were ecstatic that we were going to go to school. Nimosōm said, "Get your education and work, learn the good and leave the bad. You will live in two worlds." He explained to the kids what was meant by these two different worlds.

Nimosōm said the queen owned the school. "She promised to take care of the Indians; my grandfathers gave her this land. In return, she promised to look after her little red children by giving us education, schools to learn in, and our welfare, meaning our health. This she promises forever!"

I was curious, so I asked Nimosōm, "Is the queen at the school? What does she look like?"

"She is the richest lady in the world and she made these promises for as long as the sun shines, the river flows, and the grass grows," said Nimosōm, smiling. I thought of her hair growing forever, like the grass.

"Is she nice and will she like me?"

"She has many people who work for her," Nimosōm replied.

I thought about the queen bee. You don't mess with the queen bee because she's the biggest bee of them all. Her sting can make you sick. She ruled all her bees, so you didn't dare disrupt her home. I thought maybe the queen was like the queen bee. I felt scared and wanted Nimosōm to talk to me, to tell me everything and make me feel better.

Nimosōm said he didn't care for the queen because she put Indians on reserves when the land was already theirs, and now the buffalo were gone. "We get five dollars a year, each of us," said Nimosōm, beginning to get upset. "It was not enough in return for the land."

As a little girl, I was happy with my five dollars; I bought lots of treats with it. Treaty Day was a special day; everyone got all dressed up in new clothes that had been bought months before for this day. I got my bill from a man dressed in a big hat, red jacket, and funny pants, and I shook his hand. At Treaty Day, everyone also had an X-ray for something called TB. I was frightened of that X-ray because I was afraid I'd be shot in the back, like a deer being hunted at night. The light was so bright. As I held my breath, the lady yelled, "Take a deep breath... Hold it!" I shut my eyes as I heard the click.

Nimosōm told me about Yellow Dog Breast at the signing of the Treaties. The queen's men were there. Nimosōm called the queen's men "representatives." He said Yellow

Dog Breast was the first streaker in Canada. At the signing, Yellow Dog Breast dropped his robe. Naked, he stood in front of the Chiefs and the queen's representatives. Everyone was shocked and silent as Yellow Dog Breast stood there. Suddenly, Yellow Dog Breast yelled, startling everyone. He jumped high in the air and yelled again. Then he got down on his knees and kissed the ground. "This is my land!" said Yellow Dog Breast as he held up clumps of Mother Earth. I thought Yellow Dog Breast must have scared everyone that day with his nakedness, but I laughed at this story. Nimosōm always made me laugh so much with his funny stories!

Nimosōm said the queen was the richest person in the world because she lived off the wealth of our land now. As he spoke, I thought of the people who signed the Treaties. But I still thought five dollars was a lot of money. "Nimosōm, why didn't we stop them?" I asked.

Whenever he talked of those Treaties, Nimosōm became very angry and upset. "The queen promised to take care of her little red children and she has to keep her promise!" he said.

"*Kiyāmapi*!" Nōhkom told Nimosōm. Shut up.

Those words spoken in Cree sounded hurtful and mean. Nōhkom said his queen stories were full of shit. She said Nimosōm was talking nothing and that he should go live with the queen. I heard the word *fuck* and wondered if Nōhkom would ever learn how to say it right, with the *f* instead of the *p*. But the word *puck, puck, puck* over and over again sounded bad to my ears. Nōhkom got angry whenever Nimosōm got carried away with talk of the queen and the lost land.

Nimosōm said that the reserves would become like towns and we would have to pay a tax like the white people do, that we would become a municipality. I didn't know what that big word meant. Nimosōm said that our land was becoming empty of its richness. That the oil and minerals should stay in the land, that the moon should not be bothered. They were messing with nature, causing it to be unnatural. The white people wanted to know everything and be in control of the laws of nature; they wanted to be in control of Mother Earth. Nimosōm said that someday Mother Earth would fight back. Things were going to happen. Boys would become girls, girls would try to be boys and the weather would change; winter would come in the spring, rain in the winter, and summer in the winter. There would be different kinds of fierce storms across the earth. People would get sick with all kinds of diseases. There would be an infestation of bugs, different kinds coming from different lands. Finally, the earth would blow up and it would be man's fault. Man was too big for himself and brought these changes upon himself.

I was frightened and all I could think about was the bugs. My eyes became big with wonder and I asked Nimosōm, "If we have too many bugs or flies, then what are we to do?"

When my grandparents argued, the children stayed out of their way. They did not ask questions. In the silence following a big argument, the children walked around carefully and quietly. Nōhkom served Nimosōm and, in return, Nimosōm made her hot tea because he did not want Nōhkom to burn herself; her hands were too crippled to pour things.

Nōhkom slammed the plate of food in front of Nimosōm, who smiled and asked for the salt. In a way, he tried to talk to Nōhkom through me or the other children but this set Nōhkom off, and by this time she was too mad to say anything. Yet he smiled and continued to ask little questions of no importance. Still, Nōhkom would not answer.

Sometimes Nōhkom talked loudly to the children, making sure Nimosōm heard. That was awkward for me. Did Nōhkom want me to take sides? Sometimes Nōhkom told the children mean stories about Nimosōm, about how he treated her when they started living together. She said he was mean to her, making her work harder and that he ran around with a woman fifty years ago. I did not like hearing those awful stories about Nimosōm. He was the strongest, kindest man I knew and he loved me. I could not think of Nimosōm that way. I felt sorry for him but dared not say a word to Nōhkom. But that same day, at night time, Nimosōm rubbed Nōhkom's back and feet. They never went to bed angry with each other. Everything was okay again, as if nothing had happened.

One morning my little brother got up early after our grandparents had just had an argument, and the room was silent except for the pots that were banging loudly as breakfast was prepared. He sat on the edge of the cupboard in his tight briefs. He smiled, trying to be happy in the tension-filled room. "What you cooking Tootum? Toop?" he asked.

"Aw, shaddup!" Nimosōm and Nōhkom said at the same time.

Later, my grandparents laughed about it. It became the family joke, and the kids asked little brother, "What you making Tootum? Toop?" Or they'd tell him, "Aw, shaddup!" This story was told again and again and we always found it funny.

Another celebration, called Flower Day, was held every year on May 31 at the graveyard. This event also called for new clothes, which we wore proudly as everyone cleaned the family graves and placed pretty new flowers on the grave markers. Plastic flowers were hard to find and, because they reminded me of death, I didn't want to ever touch them. Flower Day was the only time I was at the gravesite because children were never allowed to attend funerals. There was always a huge feast on Flower Day and everyone from the reserve came to eat. The prayers were said by the old men. I was hungry while I patiently waited for the prayers to end, because I couldn't wait to get the candies. Sometimes I saw a box of bananas in that circle of food and wished I could have one. By the time the prayers were done, the soup was cold, but I was happy to begin eating and even more satisfied if I got a banana!

My thoughts drifted back to my excitement about going to school. "You go to school, get education, learn about the world. The white man, they are curious and they write in books. They will tell you about a different way of life, but I tell you learn the good in it, okay, Ceecee?" Nimosōm said to me.

"Nimosōm, I will take the good, but will that queen lady be there?"

"Maybe you will see her someday," Nimosōm said.

My mother and grandparents got us ready for boarding school. Nimosōm sold more pickets, scrap metal, my baby teepee, and my violin; he borrowed more money to dress us in new clothes for school. Aunt Verna, my mother's sister, helped to buy things because she worked. Aunt Verna told me about her first job at a farm where she made eighteen dollars a month. I thought that my aunt was like a nanny in the movies who helped my grandparents care for all the kids.

Before I left for boarding school, Nimosōm and Aunt Verna purchased me a new light blue coat and matching blue hat. Nimosōm said the queen dressed like that. I had new underwear, a new dress, and new shoes. Aunt Verna gave me a matching light blue suitcase with a blue brush. The suitcase had a mirror and tiny compartments. It smelled pretty, just like Aunty Verna. I felt beautiful and regal; this was how the queen must have felt all dressed up in her blue hat and coat.

Once again, I asked, "How does the queen look, Nimosōm?" as I watched Nōhkom pack my suitcase with some goodies and the blue brush and hand mirror. My long hair hung down my back. Nōhkom wanted to cut it a bit so that I didn't sit on my hair at school but I grabbed my head and pleaded, "Nooo." When my mother was home, I cried when she brushed my hair because she was rough with the brush, pulling my hair back so tight that my eyes were almost shut. I yelled at her to stop.

"Pōyo! Kikāwiy ana. ēkawiya ē-ko-si-isa Kitos. Namōya ē-ko-si ta-pikiskwatat," Nōhkom said. *Stop it. She's your mother. Don't speak to her that way.*

"Nimosōm said I can do it by myself," I replied as I started to cry.

My mother took many pictures as we left for the first day of school. I felt sad yet I was excited to go to school and especially to meet the queen.

GOING TO SCHOOL

THE RIDE TO THE BOARDING SCHOOL WAS VERY long. I wondered who would be at the school. "What will I learn, Nimosōm?"

"Learn all the good, leave the bad," Nimosōm said. I wondered what he meant by bad so I asked him the question again. "You will learn how to read and write," he replied.

"Will you come for me?"

"Yes, I will come visit and you will come home for holidays—Christmas and summer," Nimosōm said. I felt lonesome already.

"Will the queen be there?" I asked. No one answered. "Am I a red child?"

"You listen in school and learn. Go to her school, her people will take care of you," said Nimosōm.

I was proud of my light blue matching coat and hat and my little tiny light blue suitcase. I felt pretty and important, like a queen. *This is how the queen of all the lands must feel. I hope she likes me,* I thought.

The school was a red and brown brick building; it was big and scary and smelled like dough inside. The floor was all concrete. When my family and I arrived, a black and white thing appeared and walked toward us. It was a woman in a long black and white dress that covered her head; her face was very white and she wore round wire glasses. A black necklace with a cross hung around her neck. "Hello," she said, "my name is Sister." I thought she might be the queen's sister.

"She is a nun," whispered my cousin, Kaya, who was in a dorm for older girls.

The nun smiled at us; she looked very kind as she explained, "Myrtle will be in the little girls' dorm and I will look after her." The nun took my blue suitcase and my hand. When I looked back, my family was gone. I began to cry.

The nun took me down a long hall to a big room with a cement floor and lots of small cupboards that sat one on top of the other. Suddenly, she stopped and said to me, "Get out of these dirty clothes!" She locked my suitcase up high in the cupboard and threw a dress and apron at me, hissing, "Put these on!"

I was shaking and I cried out, "Nōhkom, Nimosōm!"

A hard slap landed on my head and whipped across my face. The nun kneeled down and shook me. "Don't you ever speak that pagan tongue again. Do you hear me, do you hear me?" Her face grew red as she yelled at me. I felt the fear move through my little body. My arms felt prickly and my legs couldn't move. I felt frozen as terror shot through me—I was turning numb with fear. I cried louder, screaming as the nun slapped me again while jerking me back and forth by the hair.

"You little ugly dirty Indian. Change your clothes. You stink like a savage!"

I felt the nun's spit land on my face; her breath smelled of decay. I wanted to vomit; I gagged and could not breathe. The nun continued to slap me as she yelled at me about my "evil tongue" and my "ugly dirty clothes."

I could not stop crying and shaking. "Stop crying, you little dirty pagan, or I will give you something to cry about!" The nun slammed me so hard against the locker doors that I fell to the concrete floor. The nun looked as big as a giant looming over me. She pulled me upright by the hair. I changed my clothes, trying not to cry. My heart pounded and my head throbbed with pain. The sobs stuck in my chest, making it burn like fire. The tears rolled hot down my cheeks. I tried to blink them back, but they kept coming, gushing like a spring from underneath my closed eyelids. My cheeks stung, burning from the slaps. I tasted the tears on my lips; it was like drinking tears from a cup. I could not stop my body from trembling.

The nun had forgotten to put my blue coat away when she took the blue suitcase. "Let's put this ugly stink coat away and out of sight," she said as she locked my blue coat up high in the cupboard along with my other clothes and my pretty blue suitcase. I continued to shake with fear.

When I was fully dressed in the clothes the nun had thrown at me, the nun took me to a big room full of little girls like me. They stared at me, watching as the nun sat me on a chair and put a towel over my shoulders like a cape. She began to cut my long hair.

As the nun buzzed the back of my head and poured some liquid that smelled like gas onto my scalp I thought of Nimosōm and what he had said about my hair. My forehead, ears, and neck burned from the liquid. It felt like the nun had set me on fire. All the while, the nun slapped my head and yanked my hair. "You are shameful; your hair is full of bugs."

My hair lay on the floor. The nun called a girl to come and sweep up "this dirty hair." The girl came and did as she was told but did not look at me. She took my hair and put it in a garbage can.

My heart broke for Nimosōm, for myself, for my hair. No one had ever touched my hair and thrown it away like that. My heart broke as the terror pulsed through my body. I finally stopped crying but I continued to shake uncontrollably, gasping for air each time the nun hit me. My nose was bleeding; the nun laughed at me and called my blood "pagan blood."

I saw Kaya moving her lips, silently saying, "Don't cry." I wanted to scream for Kaya, cry for her to help, but instead I sat quietly, as I looked at her. It was a comfort to look in her eyes. I stayed focused on Kaya as she smiled at me. I still had blood leaking from my nose but I remained calm as I watched Kaya's eyes, watched Kaya smiling at me so peacefully. I held my quiet jerking sobs in my chest as my head was shaved at the back.

My heart beat fast as the fear continued to spread and settle deep within my little body. *I want to go home. Come and get me please. Please take me home now.*

THE LITTLE RED CHILD

At the boarding school, I saw Mavis, one of my cousins, who was a year younger than me. Then I noticed other cousins from the rez at the school. Laura, who lived at the end of the reserve, and Brenna and Geraldine all stayed in the senior girls' dorm. That is what they called the big rooms. Dorms. I was excited to talk with my cousins. But there was no talking or making any contact with family members. The boys and the girls were separated and not allowed to talk to one another. Only on rare occasions were they allowed to visit the play rooms.

Kaya left to go to the older girls' dorm. I wanted to run after her but Kaya shook her head, no. I didn't know then that we could not talk to each other.

That first night was very lonely. I was in a big room with many tiny beds for all the little girls my age. My head hurt, I had no hair anymore, and my eyes were swollen from crying.

Mavis tried to stay by my side, but we were not allowed to talk to anyone. She whispered to me that we would be beaten if we talked. I couldn't talk anyway, I was so terrified.

The nun gave me striped flannel pajamas. At bedtime, we all washed and got to eat an orange. I was given a necklace of rosary beads with Jesus nailed to the cross on it. My cousin whispered that we must pray with the beads. When all the girls were in bed and the lights were out, the nun said, "Hail Mary full of grace and Holy Mary mother of God, pray for us sinners…" over and over. It was scary listening to all the girls repeat these prayers in the dark. I wondered what it all meant, and I felt even more afraid as I lay in bed listening to everyone pray at the same time. It sounded so creepy.

I wanted to go find Kaya but knew I couldn't. *I want to go home. Please Nōhkom and Nimosōm, come get me please. I want Nimosōm's prayers. I want his songs to put me to sleep and I want to hear his tapping to the songs on the kitchen table to put me to sleep. I want to hear his whispering whistle of songs at the table and taps on the table.* How I wished to hear Nimosōm's songs. Finally, with tears still staining my cheeks, I fell asleep.

The next morning the girls made their beds, which I did not know how to do. The nun said, "You dumb, dirty little Indian girl" and threw me some gray striped shorts made of a thick fabric. I looked down after the shorts hit me in the face. "Put these on for your shower. You must wash out that stink savage smell," the nun told me.

The shorts hung down to my knees, and I noticed that everyone else was wearing long shorts for the shower. They lined up in fours and the nun gave them a bar of yellow soap that smelled very bad. Everyone rushed to the corner of the shower, and I soon found out why. I was slapped, scratched, and pushed about in the shower by the nun's hands. I didn't know that I should get in the corner, out of her reach. She slapped my head and my face and pulled at the top of my short hair.

Sister told me to scrub off the ugly marks on my face. "The spots on your face are evil, a mark of the devil." That was the first time I became fully aware of the freckles on my face. I knew I had freckles, but it hadn't mattered to me or anyone before. I didn't know it was a bad thing. The nun said she hated the evil spots scattered on my face. She rubbed the soap in my eyes and face so hard that it hurt and burned. She hit me in the nose, and my nose bled into the shower.

I cried silently, tasting the water mixed with the warm blood that gushed into my mouth as I swallowed it, gasping for air. I was choking and could not breathe. I had never experienced a shower before, and I panicked as I choked on the water and blood. Sister then sent me to pray for my sins and ask for forgiveness for the evil spots on my face.

In the chapel I knelt down and prayed for forgiveness for having the evil marks of the devil on my face. But I didn't know how to pray, and I was very frightened of the man nailed to the cross.

By watching the other girls, I learned quickly how to protect myself, and I tried not to get caught talking. Mavis and I stayed close, and if the nun caught us laughing or talking she beat us both. Soon I was the one in the corner of the shower as my group of four girls rushed to get to the back. Sister still scratched, slapped, and hit the girls if she could reach them. Every morning it was the same thing. I cried silently every morning and my nose bled every time. I drank my own blood every day. The nun said it was God punishing me for having the marks of evil on my face.

My heart pounded, my head and nose ached, and the terror I felt throughout my body quickly became a familiar feeling. I was confused about what *pagan* or *heathen* meant, but I knew that it was bad.

One morning I woke up afraid because I had wet the bed. The girls tried to help me hide it, but the nun checked our beds every morning as we stood beside them. The nun came to my bed and quickly pulled apart the sheets.

"It stinks here! You dirty Indian! Take your clothes off!"

The nun ripped my clothes off, all the while hitting me. She hit me in the nose, and it bled again. I crouched over, naked, as the nun kicked me and grabbed my hair, jerking me around the room. She ordered me to "dance naked like the savages do." I did not do as I was told so the nun beat me in front of everyone, hitting me in the stomach and the face. The nun threw me toward the bathroom and continued to hit me as the other little girls watched in horror. Humiliation, shame, fear, and cold terror rushed through me. I thought I was going to die. The room spun around. I lay on the floor, curled up in a ball, as my nose continued to bleed. The floor felt cold. I was naked. The smell of my blood was a comfort to me. I was sure I was going to die.

"Get up, get up and dance like a savage," the nun demanded again, but I could not move. The nun threw the sheets on me and said, "Wash your filthy stench off these sheets in the sink. Your body is ugly and you will burn in hell for it, you filthy pagan savage." I still did not know what *pagan* or *heathen* meant, but I knew I must be bad.

When I was done washing the sheets, the nun ordered me to the chapel to pray for my sins. "Pray for forgiveness for wetting the bed and beg for mercy that you don't burn in hell for it."

I knelt in the chapel and begged for forgiveness from the statues that looked so scary. I thought God was going to come down and punish me. I cried for Nimosōm and Nōhkom to come get me.

"I want to go home," I whispered, with tears rolling down my face.

The punishment was not over, as I had yet to see the man called the Father, who was a priest. Sister told him what I had done. Sister's voice changed when she spoke with the priest—it became quiet and kind, the way it was when Nōhkom and Nimosōm dropped us off. She smiled at the Father and left me alone with him.

He shut the door and asked why I did those things. He smiled and told me to stop being a bad little girl. The Father touched me under my panties. He put his fingers inside me. I knew it was bad. It really hurt and I gagged, but I swallowed my vomit and pretended to disappear. I searched frantically for a dot or a crack in the wall, even if it was tiny. It was a place to visit as my heart pounded and the room swirled. I froze and stared at the dot I found on the wall—I went into the dot to stop the feeling between my legs... when I was in the dot everything was okay because I was gone.

I remember waiting on the bench to see the priest when I was seven years old. A little boy came out of the Father's office, crying. Was it Kenny, my little brother? I couldn't tell. I couldn't ask. In the school girls weren't allowed to talk to the boys. I thought I had been called into the priest's office to get a strapping or a beating.

Instead, the priest touched me again.

I cried and begged him not to hurt me. His rough fingers caused a burning sensation deep inside me. I couldn't speak. He looked so scary and his breath smelled rotten.

I vomited when he finally pushed me out of his office and slammed the door. The nun picked me up off the floor and took me by the hand, muttering about dirty Indian girls and savages. I could barely walk, I was so dizzy and sore down there. I was bleeding too and I felt shame. All I could think of was going home. *I want Nimosōm and Nōhkom. Please come get me... come get me now.* I quietly cried myself to sleep that night. The nun said I didn't deserve an orange that night before bed. I didn't want an orange, I wanted to go home.

My friend and I were laughing by the lockers. The nun heard me say the Cree slang word *cha*, which is an expression meaning funny or shocking, and she started beating me and calling us all evil heathen savages with pagan tongues. After the beating, I was sent to the chapel to pray for forgiveness. I kneeled in the chapel, asking forgiveness for saying that word *cha*, and I begged God not to burn me in hell.

The next visit to the Father's office was the same torture as before. He told me to be a good girl and not to speak my pagan language. His breath was rancid, and the smell made me retch. But I swallowed my vomit as I escaped into a dot in the ceiling. There was a family in there. It was quiet and safe where no one could bother me.

The walk back to the dorm was painful. My underwear was wet and I could barely walk. I felt so much shame, fear, and hurt. I knew I was dirty down there. I was sent to bed with no lunch, no supper, and no orange.

It was routine to have porridge every morning. As I poured milk in the bowls one morning, I accidentally spilled on one of the girls. The room became silent. The nun came over and hit me in the stomach. I looked up just as the nun slapped my nose. My nose bled into the milk, pooling on the floor. The nun demanded that I lick the milk off the floor.

"Lick it up like a savage!" she yelled.

The blood continued to drip from my nose into the spilled milk. When I refused to obey the nun's command, the nun grabbed me by the hair and rubbed my face in the bloody milk. I was then sent to the dorm without breakfast, lunch, supper, or an orange. My stomach hurt and it growled with hunger. But that afternoon I walked to the chapel to pray forgiveness for spilling milk and I was instructed to meet again with the Father. Once again he forced his fingers into my private parts, causing excruciating pain. I panicked and went into the dot on the wall, trying not feel what was happening between my legs.

My grandparents finally came to visit me at the school. I couldn't wait to tell them what had happened to me. The nun was so nice to my grandparents; she told them that I was very shy, but also mischievous behind her back and that I caused trouble and told lies. The nun said of all of this with a smile, even smiling at me!

I begged Nimosōm and Nōhkom to take me home. I couldn't stop crying as I begged them, but I quit when they scolded me and told me to listen in school. I missed my grandparents so much but I did not want to hurt or disappoint them. Throughout the rest of the visit I remained very quiet. I cried when they left.

At my desk, I played with a tiny strand of string and stared at a little crack in my desk. I lived in the strand; I lived in the crack. I imagined being so tiny that no one could find me or touch me. I felt safe there. I could live in the strand because I could make myself so small, no one could find me and I couldn't hear anyone. Also, I felt safe with pencil and paper. To draw was to escape from the hurt and the shame. It was safe there.

I was sent again to the Father's office. I frantically tried to reach the tiny dot on the wall so he couldn't find me, but it was too late, I couldn't get there fast enough. Later, as I lay there looking at the ceiling, concentrating so hard on the dot, I managed to leave. I got better and better at this and found that I could leave anytime to avoid that feeling between my legs when the Father prodded and jabbed. After he ejaculated into my mouth, the Father instructed me that I was forbidden to vomit the vile secretion, or I would be punished by God and not allowed to eat for a day. I was told I could leave after I swallowed. I once again disappeared into the dot in the wall. No one could find me in the dot.

I was proud that, at only seven years old, I could disappear. I could take care of myself and not feel. I didn't care if I got to eat an orange before bed. I didn't care if I was not allowed to eat for the day because I was no longer there. I didn't care anymore because I could escape from my body.

Miss Hart was the grade one teacher. She was very nice and dressed pretty in a green jacket and skirt. Her hair was red, and she wore lipstick. Miss Hart lived across the road from the school. There were times I wanted to go home with her.

I imagined Miss Hart could protect me from God, from the nun and the Father. Whenever Miss Hart asked me a question, my face burned red with embarrassment and shame. I could not say a word even if I tried. There was no voice in me.

I tried to have fun sometimes. Once, me and my friend were laughing by the bathroom. Suddenly the nun appeared and grabbed at us. She beat us, all the while calling us ugly dirty girls. I fell to the floor and the nun kicked me in the back. She kept telling me to get up off the floor. She screamed at us and told us to clean the bathroom. So we did, even though my little body was sore, aching from the ongoing abuse. This was another normal day for me.

After we had cleaned the bathroom, the nun smiled while she grabbed us both by the hair and locked us in separate lockers. The nun said we were to stay in the lockers during supper. I couldn't breathe. I panicked and gasped for air. I stood in the locker for hours, trying to breathe while crying silently. I heard my friend crying hysterically and banging on the door.

I grasped onto the memory of my grandparent's home. In my mind I could see my home on the reserve with Nōhkom and Nimosōm. I could see every room in the house and what they were doing right then. Finally, the nun let me out. I could barely walk, my back hurt so much.

The nun took me and my friend to see the Father. He punished me again. I didn't know if my friend was also subjected to the same pain the Father inflicted on me. The Father touched, prodded, and poked me with his fingers. Why was my seven-year-old body responding? How could this be possible? What was happening to me? I didn't understand. I panicked as I searched for the dot. I knew these feelings so well now and cried when I thought that it would happen again and again, as long as I was at the school.

It was my cousin Mavis who first told what happened at the school. When I told my mother, she confronted the nun, who denied it all, but my mother and my grandparents took me and my brother and sister out of the school anyway. I tried to tell Nōhkom what happened, and Nōhkom was upset at the school. Nimosōm scolded the nun. But there nothing anyone could do. The nun and the Father denied everything, and said that I was a bad girl and didn't listen or follow rules. I was only ten years old.

Sadly, my cousins, including Mavis, remained in the school. My grandparents could not take them out because they were not their legal guardians. The cousins did run away from the school a few times but were always caught as they reached the town. I was so happy to never go back there again.

The horror stories were endless. The other girls and I had experienced and witnessed so much while we were at that school. I often wondered if the other kids believed we were heathens, pagans, savages, stink ugly Indians who spoke an evil language. *Nimosōm... I never did meet the queen, but she sure had nice people taking care of her red children.*

PART THREE

WHERE IS HOME?

FRECKLES BE GONE

IT WAS SO GOOD TO BE HOME ON THE REZ! BUT when I went to the day school on the reserve, I became shy and withdrawn and fearful. All my report cards commented on this and I came to hate the word *shy*. When my name was called in class, my face went red and I could not talk because I had no voice.

I felt different and cared less about things. I felt ashamed of my grandparents when we were in the city shopping. My grandparents spoke Cree all the time, and I was ashamed of them for speaking that evil pagan language. I always looked around to see if anyone else was listening and looking; I did not want to be seen with them.

I developed allergies and asthma if I was in the bush or grass. Picking berries was no longer fun. My skin became very pale and I slept a lot and didn't want to play outside. I became sickly and frail. Nimosōm and Kōhkom Sky tried to help me; they said I had to try to be happy and help myself. I couldn't do it.

I knew the freckles on my face were the markings of the devil. So I set out to destroy them. One day I used Javex to try and bleach a few freckles but it was too painful. I didn't dare tell my grandparents about it. I tried to bake my skin in the sun, thinking that by becoming brown, I might cover the freckles. But the marks of the devil spread even more on my face and my body. Nōhkom yelled at me: "Pasiko ki-ka-kaskitē-wihkason, Mitonay." *Get up, you're going to cook your skin!* I tried a light layer of Noxzema on my face every day to cover the freckles. I thought the cream was working, but people on the rez stared at me. I had no clue that the cream was caked on my face, and that it was obvious to others, until one day a girl stared at me and asked why I wore that cream on my face for everyone to see. It looked like a mask and everyone thought I was a weirdo. But it worked for me because I couldn't see the markings of evil.

At eleven years old I started sniffing gas with other kids. We would meet and sniff from this old car in the back of the bush. We also sniffed other things, like nail polish remover and glue. When my grandparents caught me sniffing, they scolded me.

At fourteen I ran away from home for the first of many times. My focus was to get high anywhere and with anyone. I felt damaged, fragmented, broken into pieces as many men abused my body. I couldn't see their faces, but I knew who they were and, as they took their turns on me, I turned to find a dot in the filthy basement room.

I met Earl, my children's father, at a powwow when I was seventeen. At first I did not want to go but my parents insisted. My mom and stepdad wanted me to get out more often and start going to powwows. I thought my parents were trying to marry me off. At the powwow, during the Grand Entry, a guy came over to me and introduced himself. I told him to go away, but he continued to ask me questions and would not give up; he had a crazy sense of humour. Finally, I became bored with the powwow and turned my attention to this man. I laughed at his jokes and eventually agreed to go out with him.

For the next three years, I had his babies. Wade, then Isabella, then Craig. The Caesarean sections were painful. It was never explained to me why I had to have babies that way. I didn't understand when the doctors told me there were "complications." I wondered if my body was broken. After my third baby, the doctor performed a tubal ligation on me. I never knew why.

I married Earl after my kids were born, and I went to business school. My husband worked hard and tried to make a home for the children and me in the city, but I became very agitated, panicked, anxious, and depressed. I started to drink a lot, and I was on the psychiatric ward a few times for depression. My family knew the rage I carried. They knew what it was like to be on the receiving end of that rage. I had bouts of fury followed by depression. Momma looked after my kids when I couldn't. On my last visit to the ward, Nimosōm came, signed me out, and took me back to the rez, where he prepared a medicine tea of roots for the wellness of my mind. He smudged me with medicines; their scent was beautiful, healing, and safe. He sang a ceremony song and prayed. The special ceremony helped, and I started to gain confidence and feel healthy again. But when I went back to the city, the hell started over.

My children were taken from me. My mother took them into her care, and I was on a police order to not go near my mother's home. My husband left me for someone else. By this time, there were no more chances for me. I quit my business college studies. I walked around in blackouts and woke in strange places; once I found myself driving down the highway on the wrong side of the road. I had lost everything—my children and husband, my home, my job, and my self-respect. I had no one. My only consolation was that my children were safe with their grandmother.

"Myrtle, do you think you have a problem with alcohol?" asked a lady from the crisis services centre.

I cried, and for the first time admitted, "Yes, I do have a problem." I was taken to the hospital and was registered in a detox centre for a month.

Slowly I got my life back—I found a job and got a new apartment. After a year, I was able to see my children, provided I attended parenting classes to learn some parenting skills and self-help groups to build positive self-esteem. I went back to university. It was a struggle, but I didn't quit. I was determined to make a home for my children and for myself. I completed my degree and found a good job at a bank. The children came home again and I continued with parenting classes and counselling. I painted beautiful acrylics on canvas and my creative ability grew.

As I succeeded, my children succeeded. The parenting courses helped a lot. I had to live off the food bank and welfare until I was set in my career, but I found good work after finishing university, and I vowed never to be on welfare again. I wanted my children to have everything, and they did. I never wanted them to go hungry like I did in the boarding school. My home was filled with love and protection for my children. They had a good home, wore the best clothes, and their lives were busy with sports and other activities.

I looked after my children without the help of their father. He avoided all maintenance orders and was somehow able to delay the legal process endlessly. So I provided for my children with the help of my mother and my Aunt Verna. It was a struggle and disappointment that the courts allowed him to delay paying me child support. Ultimately, he did not have to pay child support at all. He was a deadbeat dad. I gave up with the legal process because it required too much energy when all he thought of was avoiding all responsibility for our children.

My mother and Aunt Verna kept us together as a family. My mother looked after the children while I worked, went to school, and took extra training. I was so fortunate to have loving, caring grandmothers to help me with the children. The children had both grandmothers and, for me, it was like having three mothers—Momma, Nōhkom, and Aunt Verna.

One day my son Wade asked, "Mom, how come you never hug Nōhkom or call her mom or tell her you love her?" I had never really thought of it before, but I tried to be more affectionate with my mother from that point on. It felt strange at first, but later became natural for hugs and kisses with my mom, and I felt gratitude to my son and often thanked him for pointing that out.

But after three years, I began to feel depressed again and slept all the time. My allergy symptoms grew and soon I was allergic to everything, including food, smoke, coffee, and even tea. Although I was slowly getting sicker and sicker, I maintained a good home for my children. I made sure they were involved in many activities. I enjoyed and loved my family so much and wanted badly to provide for them, yet something in me was not right. I had nightmares of my body burning from someone's touch. I had the same nightmare over and over. A nightmare within a nightmare. I struggled to wake up, I tried to scream, but I had no voice.

My voice had been taken from me. They took my innocence, my language, and my pride and replaced it with shame and degradation. The Father who touched me had violated my very existence. He had burned me down there, scarred me; it was hell and it seared with pain. A foul beast came into my dream. He looked monstrous. It left me with a terrifying feeling that lingered with me for days. I tried to go about my normal life, but my body ached and burned with pain. I did not know the difference between real and not real. I faked it in the real world, pretending to be well. I had to ... to survive.

I wrote in my red journal: *I was out there walking around in this pain, drinking, drugging, not really living—only existing on the air that I breathe. There is a rage inside. It can be very confusing if I let it take hold of my moment. It paralyzes me from moving on to other things throughout the day. Cry. Go ahead and cry like I never cried before. I keep crying until I can't cry anymore. I feel so wonderful and free after. I must trust me and it feels peaceful after I am done. But why am I crying? Maybe someday I will know. I will tell. But I need to cry for whatever it is ... something. Me.*

The memory of the priest and nun joggled out of my mind like a memory within a memory as I sat in my living room staring at the muted television.

My thoughts went back there, to many years ago, as I drank bottled water and breathed, listening to the whistling of my breath in the back of my throat. I was going to feel. It was real. It did happen. I read from my pretty pink journal: *I remember the beautiful butterflies. Their different colours—blue, white, orange, black, purple, yellow, brown, and violet and they flew gently before landing on my hand. I remember the butterflies so still, fragile, and beautiful. I could never hurt a butterfly ... We are running through the trails, being free ...*

That's it? I made some tea and thought, *Maybe I should sit down and write it all out. Just keep writing and writing.* But I was too lazy to write. My notes had no order. So I continued to scribble pieces of memories, throwing the words onto paper, using different coloured pens and dramatic paper colours just to be different. I could do anything I wanted. I was alone and grateful for the freedom to think.

How small I had been back then, just a little girl. I tried not to remember the sadness and the pain but only the love I had felt for my grandparents. I wondered if I'd ever grieved for them after they died, but I couldn't remember. I took a sip of tea and waited for that familiar emotional pain, but it didn't come. I smiled. *Wow, no pain.* I was tired of pain. I put the pink journal away in the drawer.

THE COUSINS

My cousins Kaya and Brenna got me to talk about the school when we were adults with children of our own. We shared our secrets with each other and talked for hours about what had happened to us. I didn't want to discuss any of it, but my cousins wanted me to do something. *What?* I thought. *It was done already. We can't change it now.* We laughed a lot at silly memories, not only the tragic events that happened.

"Why are we always laughing?" I asked Kaya.

"Because we are silly ones too, remember, but you're the crazy one!"

"You're the crazy one!" I exclaimed.

"Shut up. You are!"

"Shut up, Kiyash!"

"Shut up, Ceecee."

Neither of us liked our childhood nicknames and we teased each other about them, sometimes slamming the phone down before one of us could say the nickname—"Cee-cee," "Kiyash"—back and forth before one of us hung up first! Mine were fun crazy cousins.

One evening while driving my cousin Brenna home, I asked her to come with me to see the Medicine Woman for healing.

"Why should I? It isn't going to do me any good to bring up the past to anyone," Brenna said. She went on about just living a good life. Brenna felt that was all she had to do.

"But you're the one who wanted me to remember and reminded me of that damn school," I replied. At the end of the drive, I thanked Brenna for sharing her memories. "You girls are the ones who opened this door and now I feel alone going through this without both of you."

"Myrtle, you can do this," Brenna said.

My voice filled with emotion as I said, "Why me? Why did you bring this all up? I don't understand, so I'm not going to talk about it anymore then."

When Kaya and Brenna died years later, the whole family grieved the loss of these two beautiful women. I didn't like seeing the pain in my Aunt Eve's eyes; it broke my heart to see their mother broken. Sometimes, I still can't believe they are gone. They left this world, dying six months apart, leaving behind beautiful children and grandchildren. I knew how much my cousins loved their children. And me.

I spent years trying to work through the pain of the abuse I had suffered. I worked hard to repair the harm done to me, and the self-help groups and support from family and friends helped greatly. Yet I still struggled, sometimes daily, with living. I could not erase the scars and memories of the school. Consumed by the memories at times, I found myself living half in and half out of my life. I knew this was no way to live; I needed validation and to commit to fully living my life.

WHO AM I?

I PICKED A SKY BLUE PAPER TO READ AND THEN PUT it back in the drawer. How was I going to untangle all of it? The notes and journals had dates on them and maybe I could put them in order... someday.

One day, my mother called me. "Come over. I need to see you. It's important."

When I arrived, my mother said, "Sit. I will give you some tea. Do you want some meat?"

"Aw, Momma, you know I don't eat meat."

"You've always been different, Myrtle."

"Yes, I am, and?" I knew my mother was holding back from telling me something. Like when she busted the oil pan on my little white Datsun and told me a long, drawn-out story about how it happened. I stared at my mom now and wondered what had happened.

"And?" I raised my eyebrows.

"Here, have some cake."

"I don't want cake! Momma, what is it?"

She sat down at the table across from me. "I have to tell you, my girl, that your dad is not your dad."

I stared at her. "What?" My ears were ringing and my mind went blank. What was she saying? There was a buzzing somewhere but I couldn't see or hear. I felt faint and dizzy as the room twirled. My heart began to pound very fast. I searched the table for a dot but couldn't find one. I had to concentrate and stay in the present moment.

I heard my own tiny, quiet voice. "Momma, what did you say?"

"I know this is difficult for you to understand, and I should have told you a long time ago, but I was scared they would take you away." My mother had tears in her eyes.

"Who? Momma, who was going to take me away? Wait. Are you even my mother?"

"Of course I am your mother! Your dad is not your biological dad. He is your dad, yes, but he is not your biological dad."

"Momma, you're not making any sense."

She told me that my real dad was dead. I couldn't grasp what she was saying. "I remember him! I was thirteen years old when he died. I remember that day. I was allowed to go to the funeral because his children are my friends and I knew him too."

"That is why you spent so much time with them, and I am happy you got to know him," my mother said.

"You're happy? You're happy? No, Momma, I didn't know he was my dad! I wish I would have known this truth!"

"Well, he knew," Momma said.

"But what about Dad, my dad? Does he know?" I asked.

"Yes," she replied, "everyone knows."

"What? What about Nōhkom and Nimosōm?" I asked in a whisper.

"They all know."

I was in disbelief, completely devastated. I didn't know what I was feeling or what to say. I had to think. None of it made sense. I was not who I thought I was and the name I carried was not mine.

"How do I tell my kids? Momma, what about them? What do I say? I can't think."

"I'm very sorry to hurt you," my mom said over and over. She told me that my grandparents made her marry the man I had grown up knowing as my dad because she was pregnant. Back in the day, my grandparents convinced my mother that I would not have Treaty rights if she married my biological dad. She didn't understand what it meant to lose Treaty rights when they all lived on the same reserve. They hid me under the bed when my biological dad came to see me. My mother was ashamed to be carrying his child when he was about to marry someone else. She was afraid reserve people would call me a bastard, so she had married the man I had known all my life as my father.

"Your real dad and his wife wanted to help take care of you, but your grandparents said no because they wanted to keep you and raise you as their own."

The next day I went to see the man who I called Dad. "Why didn't you tell me you're not my real dad?"

"Well, you didn't ask me," he said.

"Why would I ask when I didn't know?"

He smiled. "You're my daughter and you always will be my daughter." That was all he said. I was furious.

I walked across the road to his mother's, Nōhkom's house, where I had visited them throughout my childhood, and asked, "Nōhkom, how come you never told me that Dad is not my real dad."

"Why? That doesn't matter; you're my granddaughter."

I wondered if my mother had talked to my family members before I had a chance. The answers they gave me were so simple. They loved me so much that it didn't matter to them if I was not actually their biological relative. After thinking this through, I was content with their answers but was still upset that I hadn't been told the truth sooner. I felt isolated from everyone and I had to make sense of it all. I needed to feel like I belonged, somewhere.

I visited my "new" siblings, who I had previously known as my friends, and told them what my mom had told me. They had already been told by their parents that I was their sister. They said they had tried to tell me, that they would drop a hint once in a while. I remembered that. It all started to make some sense but that didn't take away the feeling that

I had lost my identity. My world had been turned upside down. I wasn't who I thought I was. I just had to find acceptance in my own way, but the unknown had always created so much anxiety for me. I had to gain some control of my world, and what about my children? I had to tell them. I sat them down with my mom in the room. I wanted her to tell them. They were confused and had many questions. This affected their identity traumatically. We all cried together. I don't think they ever found an easy transition. My children were hurt, stunned, in shock. It was so unfair. But at least the truth was out. Somehow, someway, we all found a way, each of us different, but we found our way to perhaps an acceptance. Though it didn't happen overnight.

On some days, I could speak some Cree and other days I couldn't say a word. Whether the wounds were open or closed, the pain remained. No matter what was done, it would still be there. "It is like an old building," my therapist said. "Some of the bricks are strong and can be restored."

So, is that what I am? I wondered. *An old building?* I started eating the pain away, getting fat as I fed my unresolved emotions, placing a bandage on them until the pain subsided for a while. I started experiencing pelvic pain and irregular cycles, causing my stomach to swell. I hid the memories of the abuse in my stomach until my life became so stressed and complicated that I could no longer maintain a balance.

Eventually I had a nervous breakdown. During my sobriety the nightmares became surreal, and depression and anxiety overwhelmed me. It became stressful and affected my well-being and health. I was seeing my therapist about my dreams and my feelings of anxiety and panic. The day of my breakdown, fear filled my body. I was driving and thought the car was going to blow up. I stopped the car in the middle of the street and ran from it. People around me looked unreal as my panic increased. My heart raced and my thoughts echoed and pounded in my head. I felt faint and nauseated. I walked home, thinking I would never get there. I was lost.

As soon as I got home, I called Harry, Kōhkom Sky's grandson, on the rez. He came in to the city right away and gave me something to smudge my head with and talked with me until I felt safe and calm. Harry told me that a Medicine Woman was coming to the rez tomorrow. "Bring red cloth, tobacco, and whatever gift you want to give her, and get ready!"

I had nothing to lose.

I recalled the days when Nimosōm and Kōhkom Sky traded medicines and helped each other with their families. That was a comforting thought. The next day on the reserve, Harry connected me with the Medicine Woman. Plans were made for ceremony. Before meeting her, I thought the Medicine Woman would be much older but, instead, she looked young and had long, polished nails and long hair. I admired and respected her because she had the same traditional beliefs as Nimosōm.

I went to stay with the Medicine Woman for weeks in her home in an isolated community in another province. Fortunately, I was able to take time off from work and Bray, the man I was with, was able to take care of the children.

The Medicine Woman took me through ceremonies and traditional healing sessions. She did things in fours, just like Nimosōm. She took me back to visit my childhood and walked with me through it. It was as if I were working through a puzzle as the pieces began to connect within me. I was amazed at what I learned about myself and all the illness I carried from fear and trauma. I carried it all but didn't know why or what happened.

"So, which hat are you wearing now?" the Medicine Woman would ask. "What happened with you? Why did you change a few seconds ago?" The Medicine Woman called this "shifting." It was the way I coped throughout the day. It was a learned behaviour that I used to survive such childhood trauma—shifting my moods depending on what was happening to me and around me. I could shift in a second. I was so grateful and thankful that the Medicine Woman was my spiritual advisor; she saved me, and I told people about her.

As word spread, others wanted to see the Medicine Woman, so when she came to see me the word would get out fast and people came to my door or phoned to see if the Medicine Woman was available.

"Quit telling people about me, you make me sound like a freak." The Medicine Woman smiled at me as she spoke.

"I can't help it! I want to share what's happening to me with close friends."

My therapist also helped me work through the shifting by becoming more aware of my thoughts and recognizing how easily those thoughts could spiral down into hurt or fear. He taught me how to measure my feelings on a scale, to choose how much longer I would feel that way, and to trace the thought back to where it started. I learned how to adjust so easily. My awareness about how to connect my thoughts to my moods grew.

Through the therapist's insight and the Medicine Woman's traditional holistic treatment, I became keenly aware of my spirit, my shifting, which affected all parts of my emotional, physical, mental, and spiritual self. I eventually learned how to manage all four parts of myself in a healthy way. I learned how to shift my moods ten times in an hour. My allergies disappeared, and I was happy to not have to take allergy drops or shots of iron and vitamin B_{12} any longer.

So what if the world thought I was a crazy? And so what if I was! I remembered Nimosōm's words of advice, to take the best from both worlds, and I did manage to use both the white way and the Indian way to better my health. Both came together for me and the duality had amazing results. I got lots of physical exercise and went for long walks. I had been carrying around the memories for too long. In the end, it was a beautiful transformation that continued on as I grew to accept myself and became aware of myself and my emotions.

I felt like I was really living for the first time. I was seeing and experiencing life through a new lens. Understanding and caring for my well-being gave me more confidence and I was finally at peace.

But there was a price to pay.

MY HEART AND SOUL SHATTERED

EARLY ON A COLD DECEMBER MORNING A POLICE cruiser pulled up in front of my house. An officer came to my door and asked if Wade was my son. He told me to sit down and asked if anyone was with me in the house. I was weak with terror. "Don't tell me that my son is dead, please," I said.

The officer told me that Wade had died on the operating table at eight that morning. I stared at him. I didn't believe him. Shock, fear, and a slow, eerie energy moved through me. *This is a nightmare,* I thought, fear freezing my body. He asked me to call someone to come and be with me and said he'd wait until that person arrived.

My ears were ringing, and I was so confused I couldn't think. Like a robot I went to the phone and called my friend Jade.

"This can't be happening. Please come over, please, Jade." Jade didn't live very far and was there in minutes.

"It isn't real. Is this a nightmare? I can't think." My heart broke into millions of pieces. I wanted to die. Not my son. My teenage son. He couldn't be dead. I screamed for Wade. My son was dead!

I kept repeating, "Not my son, not my Wade." The officer gave me the phone number of the homicide detective and I called him immediately. I knew had to pull myself together and go get Wade. The detective told me Wade had died from stab wounds at eight that morning and that the hospital staff did everything they could to save him.

When my younger son, Craig, woke up, I told him that his brother was dead. Then I had to tell Isabella. It still didn't feel real. Jade hugged us as we cried. It was a nightmare. We could not function—our family had never experienced anything like this. The loss of my precious son ripped my soul apart and completely disintegrated my being. And when I thought of how he had died, it was unbearable—to never see him walk through that door and hear, "Hey, Mom!" My children's sadness, pain, and grief hurt me so much that all I could do was hug them, comfort them, and hold them.

Jade moved in with us for a while to make sure we were eating and that we weren't alone. Other friends also checked up on me. This support somehow helped me keep it together, but I couldn't do anything. I couldn't function. But I fought for the energy to be a mother to my remaining children. I had to keep taking take care of them. It broke my heart over and over when I looked in their eyes and heard them cry. Somehow, I had to get it together for my children. Somehow.

Wade had just turned seventeen when his life was taken. He loved it when my friends came to visit. He loved hearing the laughter, the stories. He liked to eat and loved feasts and dinners.

My mother's heart broke, too, and she cried, "Why did you go, Wade? Why did you leave?" She was devastated at the loss of her precious grandson. My mother and I comforted each other. Often the children and I would go stay at her house. All four of us slept in my mom's big bed; no one wanted to be alone.

Just two weeks before Wade left for the spirit world, he had taken his girlfriend to the airport.

"Why are you sad, Wade?" I had asked.

"Mom, I just said goodbye to Mara." Wade looked at me with such sadness in his eyes.

"Yeah, but she is coming back to Canada, right? She will be back."

"Mom, I feel like I'm never going to see her again. I felt like it was a goodbye," Wade said quietly.

Wade was quiet for days after Mara left. I knew he missed her very much. I loved to hear Mara's Spanish accent when she called for Wade. Mara barely spoke English when Wade met her, and my heart broke as I thought of Wade's love for Mara. I couldn't imagine what she felt when she called to ask me if it was true that Wade was dead. A mother knows when her son is loved. I knew Mara was the one for him. Wade's demeanour changed when he talked about Mara and mentioned her name. And now I might never hear Mara's voice either. I wished I could bring my son back, but that would never be. It would never be the same for any of us without Wade. Memories of his big brother blinded Craig with pain and I couldn't help him with the loss, nor could I help Isa, who cried all the time for her brother.

At first I lived each day for the two children, just to be there for them. The pain in their eyes and their cries were heartbreaking, for even I could never really know the pain my children felt over the loss of their big brother. I only knew my own pain and watched my children with feelings of helplessness.

"That is the cruel part of life," I told Jade. "To see your children suffer like that. But what can I do for them? All I can do is hold them. I can't take the pain away—they have to do that for themselves. How will they? I have to start living again so they can start living!"

It was a struggle to be a family. Sometimes it was too sad to be together, because we knew someone special was missing. But we tried to do different things together until we were okay to do the things we used to do, like having their favourite mustard steak for supper and eating brunch on Sunday mornings. But it would never be the same without Wade.

A year after Wade died, I asked two of my friends how they felt about that tragic time and they both said they had gone home and cried. That made me cry because for the first time I was aware that my friends were also grieving for Wade.

They said they took shifts to take care of me and my children. I could not remember all the details because the shock of losing my son had frozen me, leaving me unable to cope, often numb and motionless, sometimes screaming and crying. I thanked my friends for being there.

I sat down at the table and wrote a letter to my son and begged God in the letter. My heart was breaking, and I cried for my son. *To hold you again, my son, to kiss you, to hear your stories of the day, I want to hug you, I want to see you, to have you home here. God, please take care of my boy, please love him, please comfort him and hold him, please, I beg you, God, from my soul, please protect my son. My Wade.*

THE CONNECTION

THREE YEARS AFTER WADE'S DEATH, THE FOUR men accused of killing him stood before a judge. They had been convicted of manslaughter and were being sentenced. Three of the four received two years, but one was sentenced to just one day. One day for stabbing my son how many times? Thirteen times. I could not believe this was happening.

It seemed like a big game to the lawyers. The men who killed my son had lawyers who edited my victim impact statement prior to reading it before the court. It felt like the cruellest re-victimizing ever done to a mother who has lost a child by homicide. The Crown prosecutor allowed only two victim impact statements from two of my family members. This was not right. It was unfair. I had been treated unfairly from the start, when the police and hospital did not call me right away, even though my contact information was in Wade's wallet. They knew who Wade was, and yet I had received no call. I could have gone to the hospital if I had known he was in there all alone. Wade died alone, and I would never get over that or forgive the police and the hospital.

There was no support for me and my family during the court process. I requested to sit in a separate room while waiting for court to start and during breaks, but I was ignored. Instead, I had to sit with the families of the men who killed my son. My calls to Victim Services were unanswered.

The judge did not respect my son's life. He allowed the accused to smirk and snicker at me and my family throughout the court hearings. It was intimidating, threatening, and disrespectful. My family asked the Crown prosecutor to talk to the judge and the defence lawyers about the accused's behaviour, but our concerns were ignored. In the end the judge's sentencing orders sent the public a strong message that clearly said it was okay to kill.

The entire criminal justice system in that town victimized me and my family. The four accused were on probation conditions set out by the courts when they took my son's life. One was even a known dangerous offender. The police said Wade was at the wrong place at the wrong time. If the judges and probation officers had done their jobs, perhaps my son would be alive today.

Wade had been visiting another town. He had told me he was going on a trip and was to return early the following Sunday. I wondered about all the people who worked in the justice system who had made the decision to keep his killers out in the community, out on the streets, ignoring their curfew. Do they sleep well? They are responsible for my son's death too.

I imagined them feeding their families on the salary they made. Salaries that came from making decisions to release offenders back into the community after assessing their risk to reoffend on a grid, letting them out of jail to kill innocent people. I wondered if they ever thought about the families who had lost innocent loved ones, young ones. I thought, *The men you allowed back into the community were stabbing my son while you dreamed nice dreams in your comfortable beds in your safe home.* I wondered if someday the judge and justice workers would have to answer for their decisions. I wondered if any of them experienced the karma that I believed was coming their way. Maybe they wouldn't in this world, but maybe the next. I was exhausted with grief for my son.

Part of me wanted to fight against all of the unfair processes, but how far would it go and who would listen? The investigation had been poorly done. I wrote letters, but no one answered. The subtle racism of the criminal justice system seemed to serve a purpose for only certain people, people who get to call a lawyer right away, people who are accommodated with proper victim support and even compensation. These people get an acknowledgement and an apology. I heard about the justice system flying in families from other provinces to attend court hearings in other jurisdictions. All costs were paid, but of course, those people were not First Nations, so they were treated better than my own family. I felt strongly that the system in that town was totally responsible for my son's death. *If I were white,* I thought, *I could sue because that is what white people do, but First Nations people don't think like that.* "It is not going to bring anyone back," the Elders say. But why couldn't I sue the system? Why don't more First Nations people do that? Because it is harder for First Nations people to sue, to make someone accountable, and it takes many, many stressful years, and even then, you might not win.

The old people told me stories of life after death and how beautiful it is and how much peace there is in the spirit world. Sometimes I felt the peace, and sometimes I felt the love and warmth, and it was more than anyone could imagine. I could only get glimpses of it, but it was enough to give me strength and hope to carry on and wake up each morning. I sometimes forgot about the anger and felt the peace. People that have been through similar tragedies told me that it takes time to heal. I did not believe that "time heals all wounds." I knew I would never completely heal from this tragedy. The loss of my precious son was a wound that could never be healed. But somehow I was able to live and cope. Somehow.

Following Wade's passing, a friend of mine told me that every night she arranged a prayer circle with her friends; they would phone one another at a specific time and they would all pray for me at the same time in their own way. I am sure the prayers helped me. They did this for quite some time. Maybe the prayers carried me through the tragedy, although I did not know it at the time.

My life was divided by everything that came before that devastating December day and everything that came after. I was no longer the same person. People who have lost a child in a violent way know exactly what I mean. Those who have never experienced a loss as tragic as losing a child said things like, "I can't imagine what it's like," "You are so strong," "I don't know what I would do if I ever lost my son," "God needed him home," or "It was his time." I wanted to scream, "You don't know, so stop talking and don't say anything at all!" but I knew they were only trying to give me some comfort with these words, so I didn't say anything at all.

One evening after Wade died, I overheard my teenagers talking. "I think Mom is depressed," Craig said. "All she does is come home and lie on the couch and watch TV. She doesn't go anywhere."

Isa replied, "Yeah, and she sends me to the store for Pepsi all the time. Remember Ali's mom? She was depressed, always in her robe, never worked, and sent her kids to the store for Pepsi all the time?"

"Yeah, but Mom dresses up and goes to work."

Isa said quietly, "Mom is depressed."

"Yeah, I think she is too."

I knew Ali's mom had mental issues. But I didn't think I did, so this discussion alarmed me. I had to snap out of this and get a life.

It was an overnight change. I signed up for advanced art and sculpture classes and began creating new pieces. The art classes brought out my creative side. Making art took me from down mood swings into a bright world of amazing abstract forms and colours. The advanced classes were just what I needed to move myself out of that black hole of depression and complacency.

My anger, a tremendous, deeply rooted force, continued to make me lash out at the nun, the priest, the school, the Church, and the government. To calm myself, I drank tea that was made from special roots. I was troubled with rage and unsettling thoughts, so to help ease my spirit I wrote:

> People are not accepting responsibility. The First Nations people are a hot commodity in society. They are the bread and butter for the table. The government makes a good living looking after its red children. The queen and her representatives are the power. Indigenous people continue to support them by putting needles in their arms, eyes, neck, and legs, staying drunk and stoned, beating their wives, husbands, and children, staying uneducated, living in poverty. We kill each other and keep the jails full because without us there would be no programs or institutions that create employment and retirement benefit packages. Stay a victim because they need us to survive. Without us they will have nothing. They need us to be the victims. The economy will suffer if we get well. Imagine what this would do to society. Surely the economy would fail. Jails would shut down. How many peoples' lives would that affect? Doctors and

pharmaceutical companies would go broke. There would be a starving society.

I will... condemn and slaughter to pieces... all of you, for all the damage you have done to a nation. You perverts, rapists, and molesters, you language stealers, you voice takers, you killers! Shame on you! You take back all the terror, pain, humiliation, shame, racism, guilt, embarrassment, molestation, and rape!...

To all the residential boarding schools, the priests, and the nuns—I'll forgive you over and over and then I'll take it back over and over. No way will I forgive you. When will you pay for what you did? How can you take this all away? Make it like it never happened. Where is the karma? What you've done to a nation, to me, to families that live on today. The Red People live in genocide, in cycles of shame, poverty, killing each other, many forms of self-abuse. Men are buying young girls and boys on the streets. The men pay them for sex, for blow jobs. And no one is saying anything... still silence... shhh... leaders turn the other way...

I wrote this on a piece of white paper and put it away in the drawer where I kept all my secret writings.

PART FOUR

NO QUICK FIX

NO LOVE HERE

ALL THOSE YEARS, I TRIED TO HEAL THE PAIN with doctors, food, cigarettes, shopping, money, counselling, alcohol, drugs, men, sex. Men and sex, yes, many relationships.

I had hurt my children the most. I was not proud of what I had done to them. I had been a young mom, overwhelmed and not emotionally present for my children. I abandoned them. Back then I was living in my addictions, putting them before my children. It was a blessing that my momma took them from me. I was wrong to leave my children when they needed me to nurture, love, and protect them.

People said the same clichéd phrases to me. "Forgive yourself" or "don't be so hard on you." Those phrases kept me stuck and sick inside. I took a slow, deep breath, thinking, *Fuck you and fuck off with your clichés. Whose words are those? "Forgive yourself… Don't be hard on yourself." Stop saying that to me. This is what I have done and I can never undo it and I will live with this forever. I will remember forever the wrong that I have done.* Tears welled in my eyes. *If I want to remember, then so be it. I will hurt over it for the rest of my life and that is just the way life is for me. That is my reality. I have a choice if I want to bring up memories of hurt and guilt. I have a choice to be hard on myself yesterday, today, or tomorrow.*

I believed I had broken an unwritten law and now I had to live with it the rest of my life. Yet, since accepting that I broke this law, I found that I could live for the moment. Only my Creator knows what the final outcome will be for me. I abandoned my children, my precious babies. I traumatized them, their little spirits, and abandoned them. For me to ignore or deny it was not being responsible. I would say sorry forever to my children. I couldn't change the past but at least I could try to move forward somewhat, and so could they. Had my children reached their own point of forgiveness? Had they even thought of it? I didn't know.

Nimosōm once said, "Those babies aren't yours to keep forever. They are loaned to you from the Creator. They are gifts. You must honour and look after them. It is a law though it's not written, but it is known. Never hit your child and look after your child, or your child will be taken from you someday."

I jotted down a memory in point form on fuchsia paper. I would put it in my journal later. I took a full, deep breath that went searching through my body. Inside was pain, the pain

I couldn't put away for later. I am connected to the trauma once again.

After I finished writing, I placed the note at the very bottom of the drawer and shivered. I was happy I didn't feel the pain in my heart or experience a headache from the memory that I stored somewhere inside me so long ago.

When I was twenty-four, I broke up with my children's father and later moved from the rez and went to live with my boyfriend, Ned, in the city. After a night of partying with friends, Ned and I walked back to the apartment we shared. Suddenly he became enraged. I don't remember how I ended up on the ground in some back alley with Ned kicking me in the head. I tasted the blood in my mouth.

"You dirty fuckin' cunt, you fuckin' bitch," Ned hissed while kicking me repeatedly.

Ned wrapped his hands in my long hair and dragged me a bit before throwing me around by my hair. I felt the hair ripping out of my head. He spit in my face and banged my head on the ground over and over, then he choked me until I passed out. He waited for me to wake up and then he choked me again.

People walked by and didn't help. I cried silently until I passed out again. My last thought was, "I am going to die now."

As I came to, I focused on Ned, who was telling me to "get the fuck up, you fuckin' ugly bitch." I felt his fist in my face. Ned pulled me up and I staggered home beside him as he continued to slap me. I was hurt but I couldn't scream. I wanted to die.

Finally, after the brutal walk home, a tiny voice inside me asked what I was doing to myself.

Once home, Ned was tender with me and said he was sorry. He made me stay home for weeks while my bruises healed. Was my nose broken too? No one came by the house. Friends who witnessed the beating didn't say a word... *Shhh, look the other way.*

I thought Ned loved me because he was jealous enough to beat me. I had scars on my head and on my lips from the kicks and bites I received during the attack. But I still thought my scars were evidence of his love.

Bella and I were in a relationship when she went by the name Julian. Julian was my first love relationship that had felt normal. He treated me well. I was in love with him before he transitioned. It broke my heart when it was over between us.

At that time I went through pantyhose in bulk because I threw them out after one wear. But lately when I grabbed a new pair they seemed stretched and worn. I had been confused but didn't dare ask my kids about it. They would have thought I was insane! I knew that I had not worn the stretched-out nylons. But one day, I found out who was wearing them. There on the bed was Julian. My handsome Jules on my waterbed, wearing my lingerie and my nylons! *What the hell!* I was horrified, and a familiar fear swept through me as I stood there with my heart pounding. I was going to be hurt again.

"Julian. What are you doing?" I asked in a tiny voice.

He lay there curled up on his side, trying to hide. He looked so scared.

"I don't know, Myrtle."

"All this time, all this time I think I am losing my fuckin' mind over stupid pantyhose. All this time! Stupid, stupid fuckin' pantyhose, and you let me think that way! This is so twisted. You are the one who should be ashamed of yourself!"

Julian tried to hold me but I yelled, "Get out of here, get away from me!" I was frantic that the kids would hear us arguing but then remembered they were at daycare. Julian left the room. I heard the front door shut as he left the house. I cried. I was so confused.

The next few weeks were lonely. I couldn't live without Julian. I missed him so much, and I cried when I heard a familiar song: "I want you to want me... I need you to need me... I want you to love me." I felt desperate and sad, and finally I accepted Julian's call and agreed to meet him. He told me about his desire to wear women's clothing and underwear.

I told him it was sick and very wrong and pleaded with him to help me understand.

"Separate this from me and love me," he said. "Accept this as part of me. I am still Jules, the man you love. Myrtle, please accept this about me. I love you. I think of you every day. I can't live without you."

I thought about it for a month and decided to take Julian back into my life. I made him promise to never let the children see him in women's clothing and he wasn't allowed to dress like that in my home. Nevertheless, I found myself checking my new nylons and clothes every day. I felt insane. This was not normal.

One evening I went downstairs to watch television because I couldn't sleep. Julian had been working late shifts so I thought he wasn't there. I flipped on the light in the living room and there on the couch, naked, were Julian and my gay friend, Riel, having sex. I could not believe this was happening. Julian and Riel fell apart, trying to cover themselves. I could hear them as my gaze moved to the floor. The fear I felt was so familiar. My body was weak and numb and fear churned in my stomach. I wanted to vomit. I couldn't even be angry. I couldn't talk. I was frozen.

"Myrtle, I am sorry. I am so very sorry," they said.

"Get the fuck out of my house. Both of you get out," I whispered. After they left, I continued to stare at the floor until I became a part of the rug. I found a piece of thread woven in the rug and hung on to it. But the tiny little fibre did not want me to come in. I panicked, and the hurt flooded into my heart. I could not hide from it anymore. Even the thread would not let me in. The tiny thread didn't want me. My chest exploded, and I broke down and cried. I tried to find my breath but, instead, I puked on the rug. As I lay on the rug, I thought of my grandparents. *I need to go see them on the rez but they can't take me away from all this.* They never could.

I didn't sleep that night, but the following morning I pulled myself together. I didn't want my children to know about this incident. I pushed the couch that Julian and Riel had been on out the back door. No reminders. No Julian, no fucked-up boyfriend. He is not my boyfriend. No Riel, some fucked-up gay man that is not my friend anymore. Goodbye. No more friendship with either of them.

I made the children breakfast and got them off to school and then went to work like any normal day.

I went to see my mother after work to try and get my mind off Jules. She tried to feed me meat again. "When are you going to start eating meat? You're so pale and thin," she said.

My mother gave me an update about my sister being treated wrongly at her job. I liked listening to Momma talk about how white people were "always trying to keep the Red Man down."

"But Momma, she is not a man," I said.

"Well, you know what I mean."

My mother once told me, "You find out who your real friends are when you're successful at what you do. They are like crabs in a bucket, and when you're doing well for yourself these crabs will pull you back down. They go making up stories and lies and try to set up camps with others to do the same to you. Gossip. Don't ever let that happen to you, Myrtle. You just carry on and don't waste energy on these friends. Watch and you will see who is beside you and happy for you. Those are your real true friends."

I pictured these clawing crabs in the bucket. Why use crabs as an example? My mom could be so funny sometimes.

But my visit with my mother took my mind off Jules. I loved visiting my momma.

Flowers, candies, gifts, and cards were delivered to my house and my work for a week. They were from Julian and Riel, begging me to please forgive them. I missed Julian so much and my heart ached every day, but this betrayal was enough to keep me away. It was over. I listened to sad songs, cried alone, talked to my friends, and wrote love letters to myself in my journal. Self-love filled with caring, inspiring affirmations. Had I made the right decision to break things off with Julian? What would it be like if Jules was not like this and we lived a normal life together? Normal? The one time I felt true love for a man, it turned out to be so wrong for me.

One day I heard a rumour that Julian was living with a woman. I was confused and angry because I thought he was gay. I dialed Julian's phone number. "I heard you're living with this Sally woman."

Julian took a breath. "Yes, I called you, but you wouldn't talk to me. I don't want to be alone. She loves me and accepts the way I am."

"How is the way you are?" I asked, stunned at this news. I would have hit him if he had been standing there.

"Myrtle, I love women and I love making love to them, and I love men too and making love to them, but you will never accept that about me and want to be with me. And I love you very much. I think of you every day."

I didn't understand any of what Julian was saying. "What does that mean? Tell me what you mean, Jules?" The tears rolled down my face. Julian tried to explain, but I was blinded by the anger and betrayal and I couldn't hear him. I had thought I was over him, but I hurt so much as the sobs escaped from my broken heart.

That night, I knew Julian and his girlfriend were away and I broke into his apartment and trashed it. I felt insane! The next day Julian came to see me at work. He knew I had broken in and damaged some of his things but he didn't say anything about it.

"It is not my fault you are this way. So don't make me blame myself," I said.

"No, it is not your fault, but I will always love you, Myrtle."

"I need to understand. Help me to understand what is happening, Jules. I feel insane."

Jules held me and whispered, "I know, honey, I know. I am so sorry."

It took me three years to let go of Julian, but I eventually got over my heartache, and we remained friends. I gave him money, a car, and helped him with jobs. We talked a lot, but I couldn't change him. Julian was honest with me and told me he was marrying Sally. My whole world fell apart once again. I was right back in the hurt. Later, Julian and Sally had a baby boy. I once asked Julian if it was because he was white and I was Indigenous that he had chosen to marry a white woman.

"Myrtle, you can't accept me the way I am. I am bisexual and you can't accept that," Julian said.

"So, if I accept you, then you will marry me?" I asked.

Many years later Julian and I met for coffee to catch up on our lives. Julian said he missed me and that he would always love me. I didn't feel that way at all, but I was happy to see him.

"You look different," I said.

"I'm growing breasts. I'm taking hormones," Julian replied.

My eyes widened. "You're kidding me, right?" I could not believe it, but I laughed and felt excited and happy for him. "Is that for real?"

I asked him to show me his breasts, but he wouldn't. I was only curious, but Julian said he felt violated by me asking and trying to pull his shirt up to see.

I apologized. "I'm very proud of you for making this decision and coming out." Julian explained that he was transgender, not gay or bisexual. I was confused. "What is transgender?" Even after Julian's explanation, I still could not grasp the meaning.

Later, at home, I made some tea and googled the definition of transgender:

> A transgender person is someone whose personal idea of gender does not correlate with his or her assigned gender role. It does not exclusively refer to transsexual persons, i.e., those who are transitioning or have transitioned from one gender to another; all transsexual persons are transgender, but not all transgender persons are transsexual. A transgender person is anyone who fully accepts a gender identity—androgynous, hermaphroditic, intersex, transsexual, third

gender, bigender, or otherwise gender non-conformist—that does not match his or her assigned gender.

I reread the definition but I got even more confused and frustrated at my inability to grasp the meaning of all of this.

Eventually, I gave up trying to understand because, transgender or not, it didn't matter to me. Julian was still one of my dearest friends. It was the only relationship I had where friendship and respect continued. I loved that and so did he... she.

Julian became Bella. I couldn't imagine loving Bella the way I loved Julian. I tried to explain this to Bella, but I stumbled through my explanation, confusing even myself. I stared at Bella, who was in a blouse, black skirt, and high-heeled shoes, with makeup on and her nails done up all fancy.

"Sweetheart, will you stop staring now? You're making me uncomfortable," Bella laughed.

I hoped that Bella would understand someday how much I loved her, although not in any sexual way. It was an unconditional love. I was sure of that.

I invited Bella to my new home. I was so happy to have her come to visit and I wanted to talk with her about love and relationships. I was tired of the same old recipe; nothing ever changed with the men I picked.

"You have to love yourself, Myrtle," Bella said. "You're such a beautiful woman. Why do you do this to yourself?"

"But that's just it. Why? I do love myself, yet I'm still attracting men who want to change me, own me, and hurt me in the end. What am I doing wrong? Men are emotional terrorists," I said as I put cloves and cinnamon in water in a pot on the stove. I loved the scent of cloves and cinnamon and the comfort it brought to me and my home. "I can't live like this anymore. What the hell is wrong with me that I attract men who want to hurt me?"

I smiled at Bella. "I'm still searching for someone like you." Bella blushed and I said, "No I don't mean it that way, I'm sorry. I mean if you were a ... forget I said that. You know what I mean."

I shivered when I thought about Murrey. I had loved and lived with him for a year. Near the end of our relationship, unspeakable and shocking incidents occurred that I could not understand. Murrey spread his waste—yes, his feces—call it what you will. *Shit*. Yeah, shit on the walls, shit smeared on the bedroom wall, the shower walls, smeared on the bed covers. I thought I would go crazy.

"Is that shit?" I asked.

Murrey shrugged his shoulders, "I don't know."

"What the hell was that all about?" I wondered.

My friend May, a social worker who worked with children, suggested that Murrey was at the emotional level of a two-year-old and, as a grown man, he was trying to communicate at that level in an attempt to regain some control.

"I don't know of any two-year-olds that do that," I said.

May further explained that children who suffer from abuse at that age have no control, so they try to get it by acting out. That scared me and I immediately broke the relationship off. I would rather be alone than in some messed-up relationship.

A few months later Murrey called and asked me to meet him for coffee. I didn't want to go, but I really wanted to ask him about the shit. Maybe make some sense of it and to put an end to the weirdness.

"Did you put that shit on the walls and everywhere?" I asked.

Murrey hesitated and then replied, "Yes, I did."

I looked into his eyes: "You need help, man, serious help."

Murrey said he was seeing a psychiatrist. He said he was sorry; he had wanted to get back at me for being controlling and bossy. That's all I needed to know. I left the coffee shop feeling sad for Murrey but happy I was no longer with him.

GET YOUR HORSES

IN OTHER RELATIONSHIPS MEN HAD TRIED TO change me. At first they loved everything about me. They loved my creativity. They loved my excitement as I talked about my work. But then their true colours would come out. They became jealous of my business partnerships, the way I dressed, and my success. *Why would people be so cruel? Why be jealous of me? Why is it that I keep trying so hard to accomplish something in my life only to be smacked upside the head by men's cruelty?* I asked myself.

When I was with him, Bray gave me an ultimatum: "You need to decide, Myrtle. Is it going to be your work, or me?" So I chose Bray, worked less, and cancelled my art show in Germany. Bray wasn't happy for my success even though he lived off my income.

I had no recollection of ever being in a relationship in which the man totally accepted and honoured me. Instead, they expected something from me, and I would lose myself in the relationship, living only for him, totally immersed in his identity. As the love faded and the abuse started, my emotions and psychological well-being were hammered. Men all wanted something in exchange for my love, whether it was money, maternal security, or to own me like an object. The men I attracted often hid their angry and hostile personalities—that only came out later in the relationship. They had two faces. I contemplated why I attracted men like that and how it developed into a pattern. What did that say about me? Why couldn't they just accept me and be happy instead of becoming jealous, controlling, and mean. Why would they become jealous of my success instead of being proud and supportive? I was very successful, both in business and with my art, and not once had any of my men asked, "So, how did the training go today?" or simply said, "Congratulations." Instead, I was ignored and the silence continued. In the beginning they accepted my children, but when the relationship waned they became jealous of my children, my friends, my art, and my work. I decided I'd rather be happy and safe alone than be involved in another genocidal love affair.

My mom often reminded me that I should find a nice Indian man.

"Mom... show me a good Indian man!" I was tired of my mom and my friends telling me to find a good Indian man. I would date men from other cultures, avoiding Indian men, though I was keenly aware that this did not reflect well upon my culture. I wanted to meet someone who could accept me and who was also successful. I was cautious and maybe afraid too. Maybe, like me, they too wore many hats, those two-faced ones. The two-faced ones had secret lives.

What was it about me that attracted this type of man? The man with silent anger who used his love as a weapon and put conditions on our relationship as if it were a prison term to be served, all the while treating me like I was a piece of property. But in the end, it was always my fault. I would be blamed for the failed relationship. He would belittle me to his friends or a new girlfriend. No one ever knew how badly I was treated.

I met men who would say they believed in the traditional ways and honoured women, that women were sacred because they gave life, only to find out later that they didn't believe or live that way at all. They did not walk the talk; they used it to lure women, to make them believe the ways were theirs, so that, eventually, the unsuspecting woman would succumb to their lies. Who would be naive enough to believe men like that? I was, and my history could attest to it. I was searching for a man who was real, honest, and honoured himself. But how do you know? I was brought up to believe that you respect the traditional ways, and I believed this until I went to the residential school.

One day, I learned that the residential school I had attended was going to be demolished. My cousin Ava and I visited the school before the demolition. We looked at the photographs on the wall. I felt tall and brave, but at the same time, my heart ached, and I felt nauseated as my stomach churned. When I saw a picture of the priest, the Father, I stood there in a trance, shocked. My body froze completely, going numb with fear. Terror ripped through me.

Ava said, "Oh my God, he looks just like Bray!" We left the building, and I became very sick. I had lived with Bray for seven years. He had been my loving husband and stepdad to my children. Kind, loving, caring Bray, the one who left me because he was tired of my healing. Oops, correction, the one who left me for a young girl. I had felt so betrayed and the children were hurt. I cried when I was alone. I grieved the relationship I had had with Bray.

The Medicine Woman had referred to this in my healing sessions. I knew there was some connection between the two men, but I could never grasp it. At least not then, but now, as I became aware, I cried again. I should not have allowed my mind to remember.

Ava waited for me to finish what I had to do at the school. She watched me put some tobacco on the ground and pray. She said a quiet prayer for me. Then she said, "Let's go dance next weekend at the powwow. It will be healing, and we can pray while we dance." Ava and I loved dancing at powwows. We loved the drum, the songs. I would pack many outfits—one for every dance. One week I made six dresses and then could not decide which to dance in. So I packed them all. I loved being with Ava. We shared a crazy sense of humour, but Ava knew all about my other life, the life where the quiet voice comes and the pain shows in my eyes. Ava knew because I had let her in.

The Father and Bray? Bray had had some kind of perverted sexual energy when we first met. Lust maybe? I couldn't specifically describe it but I was attracted to it and thought it was love. Maybe because the Father told me what he did to me was love?

Everything was fine during the early romantic stages with Bray, but that all changed. I became withdrawn, weak, and silent but also angry at times, and I expressed my anger most violently at Bray. It made me sick to remember when Bray and I made love; I had felt so violated. The emotional pain in my chest had been so overwhelming that I lashed out at Bray in anger and had nightmares where I choked on my own vomit.

I told the Medicine Woman what Bray said when he wanted to make love and I didn't, which happened quite often. He would say, "I am not the priest, Myrtle." And I had wondered why he said that. Now I knew.

How could this have happened? How could I have picked a man who resembled the priest? Somehow these two people had a connection to me.

I should have seen the signs with my third husband, Franklin. He took me on trips, bought lavish gifts for me, and then had temper tantrums, stomping his feet, jumping up and down with his fists in the air. It was a funny picture. But real and dangerous. He had serious anger issues and was extremely jealous of my work, friends, and accomplishments. One day he was so angry he destroyed some of my sculptures. My beautiful art. He punched them, kicked them, and stomped on them. Yet I stayed. Franklin would take walks every midnight and go to the park. I was one of those wives who turned the other way and ignored all the signs. Didn't I know? People knew he was cheating on me, but no one told me.

I had taken all my furniture and appliances into that home on the rez. I enjoyed filling and sanding the holes in the wall and painting every room in the house. I put up new drapery to cover the bare windows. A year later I lost it all. It all changed in one night.

Franklin hit me and swore at me. Then he pushed me out the door and locked it. I asked if I could take my clothes, but he kept everything: clothes, shoes, and boots. I was a fanatic about shoes and boots. But when I was kicked out with only the clothes on my back, all I could think of was my grandparents, who were both dead. I had no home. Nowhere to go. I walked down the rez road to the highway.

"Come get your fuckin' horses!" Franklin started leaving messages on my voice mail about a month after he kicked me out. I hired people to go with a horse trailer to pick them up, but when they arrived Franklin yelled, "Get the fuck out of my yard. I'm calling the cops!" The next time he called, I refused to accept the calls or respond.

Franklin sold my horses. Horses have spirits and he wouldn't let me take the horses. I had no choice in this matter, but he made it look like I was the one who left them.

He would tell others they were his horses and played the victim, saying that he had no money to look after them. They were never his horses. My receipts couldn't help me because, on the rez, it didn't matter that you had receipts. I had no rights at the time, and no one would hear my side of the story. If a woman or man decides to leave the marriage on the First Nation, marital laws do not apply. The reserve land is common property, so there is no ownership. No one owns the land, so there is no land to split. So, I had to leave it all behind.

Franklin had had nothing in his house before I came along, even his clothes were old. I taught him how to dress and bought him everything. Now I wondered how I could be so trusting and stupid. I tried not to blame myself but couldn't help thinking that it was my fault that I now had nothing. I had brought all my furniture into that empty house, all of which he now guarded—the flat screen TVs, computers, and washer and dryer—like it was his. I felt used. I worked hard and lived comfortably with all the basics at my fingertips. But I was still dumb and blind when I fell in love.

Later someone told me that Franklin would tell people it was his stuff, his home. Men like him who lived off women, using them financially—it was not what I wanted. He was not an honest man. Yet I seemed to attract the type of man who didn't even have a bank account, for God's sake. Again I wondered how I got here. Why did I choose to marry a man like him? Did I think I could save him? Before I moved in, he didn't have proper utensils and used plastic forks to eat with.

My stuff was now his stuff. I couldn't blame him or anyone else. It was my choice to settle for less. I devalued myself and ignored all the signs and now I had no home and no clothes except those on my back. So, I started over again.

Myrtle, you're a sucker, I thought as I put up my brand-new drapes in my brand-new home. *Get out of my head, two-faces. Get out of my head!*

Franklin sent me a text saying his young girlfriend was wearing my clothes and shoes and that he had given her my beautiful trunk that had been made especially for me; it had my name on it and was full of special items that I wanted to keep. I was baffled by what kind of person would accept a trunk with someone else's name on it. That was bizarre.

I texted back: Well that's good. Maybe she needs new clothes and a trunk more than i do.

Go ahead and have all my old stuff. Enjoy it all. Materials are replaceable, but I'm not. You can never replace me. There is no one like me. Maybe your young girlfriend is really poor as you say; then let her wear my clothes.

He texted back: She is very needy but troubled and keeps coming to your house, Myrtle. She won't leave.

He was grasping at straws to get me to come back to him. I called his cell, but he didn't answer. I texted: That house is not my house anymore and you made that known to me and everyone else and what happens now is between you and her. So, stop texting me. Get lost creep. But he continued to contact me. I blocked him. He called me at home. He wrote letters to me and sent me emails.

"Come back, please," he said. "I love you, Myrtle. I can't live without you. I promise I will go for counselling. I will never treat you bad again."

Did he really love me so much he wanted to change his behaviour?

He took me to the city to have dinner at our favourite restaurant and then we went to a movie of my choice. He was going to change and our marriage would be blessed again. I would be blessed.

Two days later I put my key in the door and history repeated itself; the locks had been changed. I knocked at the door. I waited out back on the deck all day, wondering what I was going to do because I had nowhere to go. Finally, as the sun was setting, he opened the door. "What is going on with you? Is this one of your cruel jokes? This has to stop!" I yelled.

Rather than explaining why he had locked me out of the house, he told me that I should not dress in short skirts and high heels and that I should not talk to any other men. I was shocked. He said that, from now on, if I was going to be his wife, I must wear long shirts to cover my ass and flat shoes, no more high heels or boots. Then he ignored me all evening and wouldn't talk to me for five days.

I tried to make conversation and asked him to sit and talk about what happened. He did not respond to my requests. His best friend came over, and they talked and laughed together. When his friend left, he went back to his silent treatment. He totally ignored me.

I was numb. All I could think of was leaving … again, but how and when? I knew I had to leave soon, so I planned my escape for a time when he wouldn't be home. While I waited for the moment to escape again, this time with my clothes, I pretended that everything was okay while he continued with the silent treatment.

The tension was unbearable. I lived in fear. He was so miserable—a silent, angry energy lurked in every room. On my paydays he accused me of hiding my money and said I had better pay the bills or get out of his house. All I could think of was that I was leaving him soon. "You slut, you're so ugly and you fuck every man you see," he yelled.

As I looked around the room I realized that once again I would have to start over. This was my third time. I felt sick inside. Why had I come back? I felt used and stupid. All the utility bills were in my name, so I would have to get those disconnected. When was I going to see that "two-faces" would never change? He could never love me; he was not capable of loving anyone. I had bought him four pairs of cowboy boots and four leather jackets of different colours and lengths. *Is this what I have become,* I thought. *Is this what I base a marriage on? Buying him material things so he might love me. I'm only a mother to him.*

I wrote a note to myself, *Do not pick men who need a mother to take care of them—buy them clothes, teach them how to dress. This has to change.* I needed to stop creating the same situation where I would be humiliated and degraded in some way. It hurt too much.

Then I received threatening emails from another one of his girlfriends, saying she was going to beat me up if I didn't give Franklin a divorce. It was sad that women were fighting for that old man, a Nimosōm who didn't deserve the title. I had received other threatening emails from other women he was involved with, saying much the same thing. I didn't reply to the emails; these women had no reason to be insecure and jealous because we were already divorced. We had been divorced for a year. I felt sorry for his harem. They didn't know this man played with their minds, making it seem like they were all crazy. He loved it that women were chasing him, lusting after him. Women cried at his feet and hung on to his ankles as he threw them out the door—except me. I was beyond all that illness. The one woman he could never keep was me. The one woman he couldn't control or possess. He thrived on the drama and felt good about being a man. He felt proud and honourable. But he could never have me, ever again.

My friends and I talked about "two-faces" again and the community that applauded that kind of behaviour. People laughed and patted men on the back for having many women, young and old, but really it was a sickness in the community. It was abusive to all women. I was relieved that I was no longer involved in that cycle.

I hoped that one day reserves could make their own laws, like mediation, where each side talked things though and came to an agreement and both sides were happy with the decision. Healing happened, and fairness and wellness was granted to both sides because everyone had a say. I heard of women and men on other reserves who were left with nothing after years of investment in their homes.

It was a teen sex website that finished my marriage to Franklin in the end. I found his confirmation email that said he belonged to a site where he could order any teen sex video he wanted online. When I showed him the email, he lied with a straight face.

"It is over," I said. "I'm done, and you don't want to get help for your illness. I can't live with a man who doesn't love me and continues with disrespectful behaviour and degradation against all women. You must do it to feel power and control, to feel good about who you are. There is no honour for me in our marriage." And that was it for me. I severed all contact. This time I got a restraining order because he threatened my life after I left. I finally had some peace. Finally, there was no drama and I was happy and content being alone.

After the breakup I wrote on a napkin: *Only those that can stand up to make change can do it. Some can't and don't care to try. Or do they? They will laugh at you to your face. Or they haven't a fuckin' clue because they're in this fuckin' cycle of genocidal love. Hurt and pain is all they know. Terror, terror, that's all I know. Is that it? It exists in their spirit still trying to get out. No. It is easier to not feel. To walk around pilled-up, sniffed-up, on drugs, or drunk, or to have sex with anyone. It's easier to not feel because you can't look after the children. I can't be responsible…*

can't... can't... can't, can't, because they said I am worthless, a stink savage, an evil ugly pagan. Beat me some more. That's what I want. Hit me. Spit on me. Rape me. Humiliate me. So you will pass it on to the next generation, so they too can laugh at, belittle, and humiliate their kids... put shame on them, terrorize them, and abandon them. Their kids will do the same to their kids... genocidal love... is that what you want being the victim of genocide all the time... every day. Genocidal love will find you wherever you are!

I transferred this from the napkin to my journal because I was going to create a painting or write a song about it someday.

I woke up in my clean new bed in my clean home. I swiffered the hardwood floors over the weekend and loved how the clean floor felt under my feet.

I was sick of attracting the wrong men. Love? That was not love. I decided to call my friend just to talk about my Swiffer and I felt at peace again, enjoying my bare feet on the clean floor. Others might take for granted something as simple as a clean floor, but it left me feeling overwhelmed with gratitude.

The words flowed easily onto the piece of purple paper that I chose from the drawer: *A simple thing called choice. The cycle broken, and life begins. Is that cycle really broken? How is that life? How do you know if your life is in a mess when this is the life you have grown up to believe? How do you change that life, how do you wash away the brainwash of myths and beliefs? How do you know? Myrtle, how do you know?*

I shivered and looked for my sweater. One of my exes had always told me to put on a sweater instead of cranking up the heat. *Never mind the sweater,* I thought as I moved the thermostat as high as it would go. Damn it, this was my home.

WHAT HAPPENED IN VEGAS DIDN'T STAY THERE

Sometimes I said, "I love you, Myrtle, and you are beautiful," just to see what it felt like to hear those words. To believe them. I knew I was intelligent, and I could talk to anyone about anything whenever I felt like it. I was also the best negotiator when it came to making deals for myself when shopping or for my business. Aunty Verna said I was just like her old dad, Nimosōm. He always negotiated, and he loved to talk with people. I had a vision of Aunty Verna sitting in her hot house in her flower-print dress holding her blue tea cup as she talked. "He made good deals selling his pickets and copper with farmers and when he was shopping in the city. He bartered for things too." Aunty Verna laughed, "That's where you get that skill from."

I was definitely not selling copper or negotiating picket sales but maybe my aunty was right. I had it all—beauty, brains, a great career. Everything, that is, except love. Would I ever truly fall in love? What man would want me? What man would I pick this time? What did it feel like to be in love in a normal way? Would I even have time for a man?

It was so painful, and time consuming sometimes, just to look and feel good. But I let no hesitant thoughts interfere when pampering my mind, body, and spirit. No one else was going to pamper me.

I thought a lot about sharing this wonderful life with a man someday, but I was afraid I would never have a normal, loving relationship because I had never truly experienced it.

I sighed as I remembered the beautiful day when I thought I had found true love.

"Myrtle, I promise to look after you in sickness and in health, through good times and bad times. I promise to be faithful till death do us part. You are a beautiful gift the Creator has given me. You are a gift of love... Myrtle, I will cherish you forever..."

I could not believe this was happening to me, a dream come true. After many failed relationships, I was finally in love with the perfect man. I was full of joy as I listened to my handsome groom speak his beautiful vows to me as tears rolled down his face. "Oh my God, is he crying? Is he really crying for me?" I wondered, feeling somewhat embarrassed for him but smiling because I was ecstatic that this moment was really happening. "I love you so much, Blake," I said.

The minister turned to our family and friends. "Ladies and Gentlemen, I now introduce you to Mr. and Mrs. Smith!" In my head I said my new name. *Myrtle Bernadette Smith, Myrtle Bernadette Sage River—Smith.*

The crowd cheered and congratulated us. Suddenly fear shot though me, but I tried to ignore it as I listened to the cheers. The fear startled me. I scolded myself, *Act right, for God's sake, act normal and go away, fear, go away.* My face was getting sore from smiling. We signed the marriage papers with our dearest friends as witnesses and then we were off to the valley for a photo shoot by the lake. The diamonds in my wedding ring sparkled in the sun. My life was filled with happiness, contentment, and love. Mrs. Blake Smith. I felt blessed. It had finally happened—I was married to the perfect man.

Five years passed. Our special happiness didn't last through the years. Everything changed. Blake kept me isolated from my family. My husband subjected me to days of silent treatment and psychological abuse, and I felt controlled, tired, and beaten.

One day Blake pushed me out the door with nothing. He called me names and spit on my face. It was my payday and he accused me of holding out on the money and giving it to my kids again. "I will give you all my money. Don't hurt me anymore please," I said. That night I stayed outside on the deck and prayed for Nōhkom to come get me. *Take me home, please. I want to go home.*

The next day I knocked and called for him to open the door. I banged on the back door for two hours. I screamed through the door, "Why?"

Finally, he opened the door. "What is going on, Blake?" I whispered, my voice hoarse from yelling at the door for what seemed like hours.

After a lengthy silence, Blake responded, "I thought you left me."

"What?" A tiny fear, like a spark in my stomach, made its way through my whole body. I was so afraid of him. He started to cry and he wouldn't talk to me. He did not talk to me for a week. His best friend came by and they laughed and smoked cigarettes, had coffee and a good visit. As soon as Blake's friend left he went back into his brooding, silent, angry mood. He slept on the couch.

I begged him to talk. He wouldn't even look at me. Instead, he watched TV and lay on the couch, ignoring me. If the phone rang, he didn't answer it. I lived in total silence and every day felt sick to my stomach with anxiety, confusion, and fear. Finally, after two weeks I left.

Even after I left, Blake still had my heart somewhat. He had deliberately sent another woman an email, repeating the words of the wedding vows he said to me on our special wedding day. That day was clearly etched in my mind—the quivering of my husband's voice as he read the sacred wedding vows and how his tears rolled down his face. After reading the email, which popped up when I logged on to the computer, I felt betrayed and knew my marriage was nothing but a lie. How could I not have listened to the voice inside me that said this man was not the one for me? My wedding day had been one of the happiest days of my life, but I had to trust myself to see the truth as I reread the email.

You are my gift from the creator. You are a gift of love. The creator brought us together. We are meant to be together. Another email read, *I am traditional man of the lodge... brown and handsome.* Oh, how the women fell for it.

But I had lost everything. *Don't you ever learn!?* I thought. *No more, no more Indian men, no more craziness!*

The doorbell rang repeatedly—only my friends rang the doorbell like that. I ran downstairs to open the door and yelled, "I'm not going. I told you!"

Dee and Samantha came in and glanced around, before Dee finally asked, "Are you hiding a man in here? I hope you're not back with Blake, Myrtle."

"Are you nuts? He is the furthest thing from my mind," I said.

"Well, don't go back. Hang up on him if he calls, and don't answer his texts or messages. Did you block him?" Dee said.

I stuck out my tongue at Dee, but she ignored me. "If you go back to him, Myrtle, I swear to God we are going to go to that rez and drag you out of that house."

My friends had come over to invite me on a road trip to the next town to buy vibrators. They were divorced and single and, despite that I had been divorced too and was well versed in the matters of sex, I felt silly about the subject of vibrators. "No, I'm not coming. Why can't you all understand that?"

"We have to break that residential school shame out of you and all the evil taboos about masturbation," Sami said.

I felt my face going red. "That's not the point. It's my own decision, and I just don't do that to myself with a thing."

"You can't even say it. What thing? Just say it. You can't even say the word!" Dee shrieked.

"Vibrator. There, I said it."

"And why do we need a vibrator?" Dee asked, urging me along.

My friends watched and waited for me to answer. "I'm not embarrassed. You girls are making me feel silly. Why do I have to say it, and I don't even want one?" My friends waited in silence. "Okay then, you need a vibrator to poke yourself with!"

"Oh gosh, unbelievable! What do you call what's between your legs?" Samantha asked.

"A vibrator for your spoons?"

"That's it, it's no use. See, she has that old nun mentality, old residential school mentality. She's brainwashed so badly," Dee said.

"I am not," I said. "All right, I will tell you. You are driving to the next town to buy vibrators, so you can please your *v*'s in your spare time until you find a man, and you want me to come along and get one too so I can poke myself to pleasure."

"Vagina! Call it a vagina, and the word is not *poke*," said Samantha.

I laughed. "You women are so funny—wannabe sluts in your more mature years." They clapped their hands. I wanted them to leave so I could be alone and enjoy my new home. My friends did not realize that I basked in the peace of being alone. I loved not having Blake's misery and anger lurking over me. "Nope, not going, and why are you going to the next town to buy vibrators, anyway? What are you all embarrassed of?"

During one of our walks, I had told my friends that I often thought my loved ones that had passed on into the spirit world would see me pleasuring myself. I didn't think it was right and in my mind and soul I felt embarrassed. They disagreed with me, but I explained that it was my belief and that I didn't get off on that kind of thing anyway. "Happy orgasmic day to my crazy friends," I said as they left in search of their vibrators.

After that, whenever I called them and they didn't answer, I thought they might be busy masturbating. I left messages on their voice mail: "Hope I'm not interrupting your poking event this afternoon, but give me a call after you have your orgasm," or "By the way, how many orgasms did you have today?" Sometimes I sent a text: How are the batteries? Call me later when you're finished.

My friends thought I was missing out on the best sexual experience a woman could have by herself. But Blake had talked about masturbation. "Don't forget the unwritten laws when you do that to your body. There is a price to pay when you sexually please yourself," he said.

"You are kidding me, right?" I was stunned.

I realized later that Blake was trying to control me just in case I thought of pleasing myself. I knew what he said wasn't true, that it was an emotional game he played with my mind, trying to instill fear in me. He wanted me for himself only and that was one way of maintaining control over my mind, body, and soul.

Once when Blake and I had gotten back late from a trip, I rushed to a meeting the next day, forgetting to remove Blake's nose hair trimmer from my bag. The meeting had already begun when I arrived and placed my notebook on the table and my bag at my feet. At one point during the meeting something started to buzz quite loudly under the table. Everyone, including me, looked around the room wondering what the whirring noise was and where it was coming from. We were quiet as we listened. As the room's attention focused on me, my face reddened as I realized it was Blake's nose hair trimmer! I leaned under the table, felt for the trimmer, and turned it off. I was so embarrassed!

"What is that, Myrtle?" the manager of products asked. I didn't say a word and stared at my notebook while I listened to the laughter and whispers. It was one of those situations where it was best not to say anything at all. I didn't want to explain what it was. I could only imagine what they were thinking. "Does she shave her nose hairs?" How embarrassing!

That night I told Dee this story and we laughed about it. "You have got to be kidding me, Myrtle; maybe they thought there was a vibrator in your bag!" Dee said.

Not once had the thought entered my mind—I had never even heard the sound a vibrator makes. "Is that how a vibrator sounds?" I asked.

Dee laughed, "Myrtle, you're so naive but I love you!"

I was pretty embarrassed, but I laughed too because I really was naive. Not long before, I had asked my friends if they had ever experienced an orgasm. Some of the women who were half a century old had not. I could not imagine that some women had never felt that sensation.

Blake was in relationships all the while keeping me there. He did everything to stop the divorce. I had married someone who was out to destroy me, to kill me. That was not love, this is not love. It was emotional terrorism once again. I panicked when I realized I was attracted to the same type of man over and over.

"Do normal people think like this?" I asked Samantha. "This is a fuckin' nightmare and I am sick and tired of it all. Who did I marry? I don't know who this man is." She encouraged me to go back to counselling; maybe there was something more I needed to take a look at. Marriage should not be this complicated. It was not normal; it was exhausting and scary.

That night I prayed to Nōhkom in the spirit world to help me. *Protect me. Is this what it's like to be married on the rez? If not, please get me out of here. Please. If I have to walk away, help me to be safe while I walk away. Nōhkom, please help me. Come and get me. Please.*

When I was still with Blake and away from home on a business trip, I got a text from a guy that read: can you send me a picture of your tits? Always one or two married men tried to proposition me when I was at conferences. I considered texting back: Is your wife sitting next to you right now? And how many other women are you texting?

It always made me feel so violated and pissed off!

Why did I get these texts? This was not the first time or the same man. I shut my cell off. I was exhausted and had to give a presentation to a group of Indigenous business leaders and Chiefs the following morning.

Blake called my room and I told him about the men and their text messages. "They were probably drinking," he said.

"Do you think they know who they're texting?" I asked.

My single friends got the same kinds of texts from men they worked with. The women never complained or told anyone about it. Why were these men protected? I only gave my cell number out for business purposes, and I was shocked that men behaved this way. There was so much betrayal going on out there. Married men texting women and cheating on their wives while on trips. Everyone knew about it, yet these men got away with it because they had so much power. They had two faces. There were many people with two faces, and their behaviour was accepted by silence. And yet everyone knew. Everyone except the wives—or did they?

I wanted to call up the wives and say, "Your husband just came on to me and other women again on this trip while you're at home with the kids. Maybe 'two faces' left you at home this time so he can get something new and exciting on his trip. Check his cell phone and see who he is texting."

Nōhkom used to talk about men like this in her broken English. "Man that run away on their wife and have lots women. They are dirty. They not clean. They not think nice of you and they live two lives, show two faces."

My friends told me which men were texting them and who was sleeping with whom. People talk in the communities, yet no one tells the wives. My friends told me who wanted sex from them, but they had too much respect for themselves and would never step out with a married man. They talked about the two faces.

I know there are good men out there, respectable men who have been married for many years and honour their wives, their families, and their communities. There are good leaders out there who are very honourable and respect women. They never step out on their wives. They have respect in their lives. And it is visible who these men are. They are great men and great leaders. They walk their talk. They really care about their reserve and the people in it. Their communities are growing in economic development and more youth are graduating and accomplishing their dreams. They are successful, and the community is successful.

I shared all my secrets with my lawyer friend, Kane, because I knew I could trust him. When I told him about the text messages, he laughed, "Let me at them. I will rip them a new asshole."

I giggled but then looked at Kane with seriousness and asked, "Kane, what is it about me that attracts these men and where is the respect?"

Kane smiled. "It's not your fault. It's just that you're very beautiful."

"Yes, okay, then why don't I attract the nice guys?" I stared at his suit, noticing his shiny gold cufflinks and wondered if they were made from real gold.

"Myrtle, let it go. These men are sick. It's like an illness when they are out on the road, and it's all about power and control, and they abuse it. They don't respect women." Kane shook his head.

"It bothers me so much that I can't tell them to stop or tell them to fuck off. Kane, listen to me, any normal woman would do that right? So why can't I say it to them?"

"Why can't you? Just tell those sick bastards where to go, and another thing, Ms. Myrtle, don't waste any more energy talking about them. They don't deserve you and they are not worthy of you, sweetheart."

Later, as I walked home through the park, I thought about genocidal love... *fuckin' get away from me... what am I? It is attracted to me like a sponge where pain will find me. Why follow me? Humiliate me. Yes, go ahead, text me all night... text me how much you want me as your wife sleeps at home looking after your children. You can get away with that. "Come to my penthouse," you text... Maybe I will spin into an orgasm and lose control of who I am for a moment... is that what you want... to abuse me and disrespect me so you can feel powerful... and what does that make me if you think for one second that I will accept that.*

Not long after the end of my relationship with Blake, I went to Las Vegas for an art show. My sales were great and I was happy. It had been a long time since I had felt this satisfied. I was going to spend some alone time to revel in my success. I found a table in the corner of the outdoor café and started writing in my journal.

Who writes in a journal in Vegas anyway? I threw my purple journal aside and decided to check out the casino. In Vegas, you can dress any way you want, so I had dressed past the nines. I knew I looked amazing, and wherever I went, the beautiful scent of my favourite perfume followed. I had no idea how to gamble so, instead, I ordered a margarita. Later I would try my luck, but right now I was going to enjoy a drink. The drinks were free in the casino where I stayed. After a while I decided the time was ripe to test my luck.

I looked up from the buttons I was pressing and spotted a gorgeous man gazing at me. How handsome he looked in that orange shirt. *Who wears an orange shirt and looks that good! Is he looking at me?* I was flustered but stared back. I traded my resolve not to get pulled into a relationship with a man I might not be able to trust for that spark, that chemistry I had been waiting for. We continued to stare at each other, our eyes made contact... each tracking the other's moves. He was coming over to me. I did a quick breath test and took a sip of my margarita. My heart was pounding as he took a seat next to me.

"So, are you winning, Myrtle?"

"No, I don't know what I'm doing. How do you know my name?" I asked as I continued to press numbers and sip my drink.

"I bought four pieces of your art today," he said.

"Thank you, I hope you will enjoy them," I replied, slightly surprised that this man knew who I was.

"You smell amazing, Myrtle. What is that perfume you're wearing? I caught the scent at your show."

"Bob Mackie. I've worn it forever."

Our eyes locked, caught in a trance. I couldn't remember when—or if—I had ever felt like that. Sparks! Electric euphoria as an orchestra played in the background. *Is this how it feels to be physically drawn to another*? I wondered. Was this love at first sight?

"Do you want to smell my neck?" I asked.

The man moved toward my neck and kissed me softly. He stayed there as he whispered in my ear, "I love your scent." He drew back and looked at my face. "You have freckles, and I'm in love with your beauty."

We kissed, our lips pressed softly together, oblivious to the noise in the casino.

"What is your name?" I asked. He said his name but I couldn't hear it as we kissed more. We stopped and stared at one another again. I was overwhelmed with passion and told this beautiful man that this had never happened to me before. "I just don't let anyone kiss me the way you did, and I'm not drunk, are you?"

"Come, my beautiful Myrtle, I'm going to show you Vegas!" he said.

I would never forget my stay in Vegas. What happens in Vegas stays in Vegas, right? We walked along Fremont Street for the light show, and I danced freely in the street with a margarita in one hand. He held my hand and we bought souvenirs. His limousine took us down the strip. I loved the lights of the strip. We laughed as we stood up in the limo's sunroof, toasting people with our margaritas.

Later he took me to the most popular club in Vegas, where we had a fancy dinner and danced till four in the morning. I usually avoid alcohol because of what it has done to me in the past. I knew I could be right back there in a second, grovelling in the quicksand that so often threatened to consume me. I remembered Nimosōm's words: "Always respect alcohol or it will take your spirit. Don't ever abuse it." That night, I only had two margaritas because I wanted to feel real with my new friend and enjoy every moment shared with him on that spectacular night.

I was in love! Or so I thought. The experience was one of sheer joy, so ecstatic that it was electrifying. We exchanged contact information and planned our next visit. I had a lover and he was beautiful, kind, generous, and pleased me to no end.

Reality hit as soon as I returned home from Vegas. He called and we talked on the phone for hours. I wrote my

Vegas story on a napkin from the casino: *Myrtle meets man in Vegas and...* I finished jotting down my notes and tucked them away in the drawer. He would always be my friend, my lover, but what happens in Vegas stays in Vegas!

I decided that in the future I would take risks and for once be picky. The Vegas experience gave me much to think about. I created a checklist and that checklist has kept me single for a long time. I vowed that a man must now pass the checklist test. I continued to add more to the list, but I always kept Yellow Dog Breast at the top:

Must be like Yellow Dog Breast
Be respectful
Have manners
Love children
Have fresh breath all the time
Be able to communicate
Be working (160G+ a year)
Have a car or a truck (new)
Say good things about his ex and other people
Must not have gone to residential school & neither parents & grandparents
Not have addictions (gambling, alcohol, drugs, smoking, sex, food)
Must not brag about himself
Must love horses
Must not have been abandoned as a child
Must love art shows and art

Must love travelling by plane
Must have a passport
Must know how to dress for success
Must wear nice shoes
Must groom himself regularly (no nose hairs, hair in ears, or unruly eyebrows hanging over his eyes)
Must not have bigger tits than you (My cousin Pauline added this.)

PART FIVE

THE CLAIM

THE PROCESS

ON THE DAY OF MY VERY FIRST VISIT TO SEE A lawyer, I was nervous from the moment I woke up. I paced, sat down, got up, and paced again. I had heard about people suing the Church and the government for all the hurt they inflicted on First Nations people. I felt cheated out of the normal healthy life I could have had. In the past, I did not know what a normal healthy life was, but I did now. And now that the time to start the legal process was here, I was terrified. I picked up the phone to cancel the appointment and then hung up. But after talking to my therapist and the Medicine Woman, I felt courage even though I was still very unsettled and angry.

When I arrived at the lawyer's office, I was an emotional mess. I mumbled and fidgeted, but my lawyer, Rose, was very kind and did not pressure or hurry me.

"I don't want anyone knowing about this," I told Rose. I felt vulnerable and became very paranoid and ashamed. Rose advised me to get accurate dates and names, and to write down detailed accounts of the incidents of sexual, physical, emotional, spiritual, and cultural abuse I had suffered. I did have many bits of writing scattered about my home, since I had been writing down my thoughts for a long time.

A few weeks later, I went to see Rose again to sign the claim. On this visit, I felt a twinge of power mixed with the fear, and I felt a new energy move through me; it felt good to be finally taking control over what happened.

But that night the nightmare came. It was horrifying. A black beast came into my bedroom. I could not move or scream. The black beast wrapped itself around my private parts and my stomach and proceeded to move up my body, leaving the most searing, agonizing pain. I screamed in terror. I was trapped. I couldn't feel my face and I knew I was in a nightmare. I prayed and swore and prayed, trying to wake myself up. Then I felt a jolt, and the sound of iron or metal echoed in my ears. I was awake. My body felt violated and sore and I was exhausted from fighting. I remained awake the rest of the night, afraid to sleep. The feeling of violation was overwhelming. I called the Medicine Woman, who said she would travel in from the east to see me.

But my traumatizing nightmares and terror flashbacks continued. My therapist diagnosed me with post-traumatic stress disorder, which made sense to me. There was no such thing as "closure" to all of this; I had tried everything. It was not about learning how to live with the PTSD. The anxiety was always there if I chose to let it stay. At times, it threatened my emotional, physical, mental, and spiritual well-being. Eventually, I began to make it through the day by "shifting." The Medicine Woman would ask, "How many hats did you wear today?" My emotions shifted, depending on how I was feeling about a situation or a person. I wore different hats throughout my day. The hats represented my emotions.

I wondered if, perhaps now, with my new tools, I could finally find true love with a man and have a normal loving relationship with someone special. It didn't help my confidence when I attended events at home on the rez and the Kêhtêyak, the old ones, asked me, "Ahh, Mōniyāskwēsis, who is your man now?"

"I'm alone. I don't have anyone," I replied.

The Kêhtêyak looked surprised. I knew they expected me to be with someone, like every other woman on the rez was. Everyone had someone, except me. I would, if I had shacked up with someone at age sixteen, which I would have done if Nimosōm hadn't said no—imagine getting married at age sixteen. I had been in love with a boy my age and we planned on getting married. As an intervention my grandparents sent me to live with my aunt and uncle on a northern reserve. I didn't want to go. I cried until my aunt and uncle said I could order all the clothes I want from the Sears catalogue. I loved the trendy clothes in the Sears catalogue. And when we arrived at their homestead, my Aunt Verna showed me my room to settle in. Then, at the kitchen table, she had the catalogue and she said, "Order all the clothes and shoes you want." I loved it and was overwhelmed with happiness! I began high school in the town nearby, and I loved that too. Soon I forgot about getting married at age sixteen! I dumped my boyfriend that time for the Sears catalogue, so I am thankful Nimosōm said no.

But looking back, my feelings about it were so low and full of despair. *If we'd been married then,* I thought, *now I'd probably be walking around with no teeth and only one special outfit to wear when I went to town. I probably would have had ten kids and lived on welfare in poor housing with no running water.* On the other hand, maybe I would have become a Chief who lobbied government for the wellness of the Nation, making laws to govern our own Nation, working with the Elders on the reserve because that was the only history left. The Elders are the Knowledge Keepers, the ones who know the teachings, the unwritten laws. Maybe I would have made the reserve economically independent, with reserve-owned businesses and even a cooperative business so everyone could profit from the royalties each month.

I snapped out of my dream. None of those things had happened to me, but other, terrible things had.

Done! The claim was documented at my lawyer's office. I signed a contingency agreement with my lawyer for a fee to be paid upon successful completion of her services. She informed me that the government, the priest, the nun, and the Church had thirty days to respond.

I felt brave and strong, but I could no longer remain anonymous once the documents were filed with the court. My lawyer tried to have my claim remain anonymous, but there was no way. Once they were filed, anyone could access the documents. I felt exposed, and I began to have more nightmares, horrible ones. I felt scared, like a little child again. For a week I endured pain between my legs; my senses were distorted, my thoughts were unfocused, and my ability to speak was very limited. I had to get control! *Where is my voice?*

I knew my work routine like the back of my hand but it took every bit of strength in me to do it. I felt vulnerable and exposed, as though everyone in town and at work knew that I had filed a claim against the school. My stress and anxiety continued as I tried to maintain a sense of normalcy in my daily life.

Regardless, I had to continue and to get my work done. I made many mistakes. My hair extension fell out in a meeting, and I was embarrassed and ashamed. I was flustered and wanted to go home.

For some reason, I thought about eating meat and became nauseated. I couldn't stand the smell of meat and my eyes watered at the thought of eating it. I thought I could actually smell meat at work. *I am not a meat eater. I hate meat; I want to go home, why didn't I call in sick today?* My thoughts were crazy. I couldn't wait to get out of there.

My asthma suddenly appeared again. I did not need medication because I had learned how to work through my breathing with the help of the Medicine Woman and my therapist. Yet as the body memories and flashbacks hit me, my chest began to hurt and taking a full breath became difficult. I breathed slowly, listening to my breath. It took all of my concentration and focus to stay in the moment.

I said to the Medicine Woman, "I don't think I can do this claim against the government and the Church." The Medicine Woman reminded me of Nimosōm and I listened to her words of encouragement. I knew Nimosōm would tell me, "Don't give up; face the fear. If you believe in yourself, then things will go well for you."

"You saved me from death," I said to the Medicine Woman.

"You saved yourself, Myrtle."

No one responded to the claim, and it was past the thirty-day deadline. Rose said that she would shake them up a bit, and she did.

Eventually, the government replied with a sixteen-page document stating that they were not responsible; they denied all accusations. I was very upset and disappointed as she read the lengthy document.

"This is like a slap in the face. I'm rejected and denied."

Rose said, "Don't worry; they do this all the time." She assured me that this was the government's usual response in cases like this and that she would shake them up even further until they came around. On the drive home, I was a total mess and could barely focus!

During supper that night with the children, I tried to concentrate on a disagreement that was going on between Isa and Craig. I calmly told them to settle down, but all the while I felt rage at the government for the school they put me in. *How dare they turn the other way? How dare they do this to me?* I remembered the Medicine Woman's words: "This is not an easy thing to do, but remember that you are not a little girl anymore and these memories are just emotions and you are in control. It's your choice. The memories you will have the rest of your life, but now you are an adult and no one can hurt you anymore."

That night I woke to a burning sensation between my legs, and I was very frightened, but at the same time I felt that it was going to be okay. This body memory had surfaced before. I would be okay; it was only the little girl feeling unsafe and scared. *No one is going to hurt you. I am here for you.* I slept through the night without any more nightmares.

Yes, I gained a new strength, a new confidence!

The nun's lawyer finally responded, months later, asking that I consider dropping the case because his client had Alzheimer's disease.

I was angry. "And am I supposed to feel sorry for her now?"

"We will reject that request," Rose said.

"I want that nun to remember me. She can't do this now."

That night, I went to bed feeling angry.

Rose called the following week and said that the government's lawyer had requested all of my information because they were "reopening the case."

I was confused but felt some hope. "So now what happens?" I asked.

Rose said I had to come to her office and sign papers to release all information about me.

"What kind of papers?" I asked. "When is this going to end? I don't like this."

"This legal process takes a very long time," Rose reminded me, "and sometimes it's a stalling practice, but sooner or later they have to respond because we are not going to disappear. Sometimes they hope we'll just give up, so take your time."

I felt like I was being tested. Not by Rose, but by the government.

"What the hell more do they want from me? First they take my childhood, my innocence, my language, my voice. They rape me, beat me, belittle and humiliate me, and degrade me. They are the ones who tried to kill me!" I thought about the hurt little girl, and I knew I couldn't give up.

That night my sleep paralysis and nightmares returned, and I was up all night trying to calm my anxiety. I turned on all the lights, but the moment I fell asleep, the same dream returned, one where I could not talk or move. I was aware I was in the nightmare, but I couldn't wake myself up. I tried to scream myself awake, but I had no voice.

The next day at work I was unfocused, confused, and my voice felt small. I was losing my voice. It was in my chest somewhere, but my chest and my heart hurt. My head hurt. My sentences were fragmented and my thoughts jumped about in my mind. I was tired, exhausted.

I shut my office door and called my therapist, who helped me focus on my thoughts and coached my breathing over the phone. I broke into sobs and totally fell apart as he talked to me.

"What is happening right now?" my therapist asked. "Breathe when you are talking and take your time as you tell me."

I listened to his voice and took a deep breath; my asthma was back, rattling in my chest. My therapist spoke to me calmly, telling me to follow the thoughts, to go back again. I found the little girl and cleaned her up again. I bathed her, put her in clean clothes, combed her hair, and told her that no one was going to hurt her. I told the little girl that I was going to protect her as I hugged her and told her, "I love you."

Finally, I was grounded and ready to get back to work. I hung up the phone and breathed. The pain in my chest and the asthma subsided.

Two months went by before the Medicine Woman came to see me again. Once she arrived, she observed me and asked what was going on. "You don't look well."

I said I missed Wade so very much, and I cried while the Medicine Woman encouraged me not to hold back the tears. Then she prayed for me.

The next day the Medicine Woman asked how the claim was going.

"Nowhere, and I feel like giving up. I have to go sign papers so they can investigate me, release my whole life to the government."

The Medicine Woman responded, "Good, you do that, let them see what you went through, maybe they will see what they have done."

I had never thought of it that way at all. "But I'm ashamed of my life—the psych wards, drugs, alcohol, abandoning my children, broken relationships with men, poverty, and lack of respect for me."

"That's okay. Let them see everything. Let them dig it all up." The Medicine Woman smiled.

"I don't like what comes with this legal process," I said. "There are nightmares, my self-image and esteem have taken a downward turn, the body memories are back, the sleepless nights, PTSD. I feel physical pain throughout the day and it is so difficult to be at work and do what I have to do."

"I told you they can't control you. These are feelings and you are not a little girl anymore," the Medicine Woman said.

"Will you come with me to sign the papers?" I asked her. The Medicine Woman agreed.

On the morning of the signing, the Medicine Woman was on the reserve and couldn't make it to the city on time, and I tried to cancel the meeting with the lawyer.

"No, you are not going to cancel, because you can do this," the Medicine Woman told me. I went on my own.

At the lawyer's office I sat down and fidgeted, shaking as I talked. I looked at all the papers in front of me.

"What is all this?"

"These are the release forms that allow the federal government to obtain all the information about you," Rose said. "I'll explain each one to you before you sign."

"All these papers?" I felt sick to my stomach. "There are so many. Okay, let's do it!" I said, taking a deep, rattling breath.

The rattle of breath was a warning sign for my asthma, yet I was ready to begin. Remembering what the Medicine Woman said to me, I sat up straight, like an adult, a woman, not a little girl. I remembered the spiral effect, the downward spin that my therapist had taught me to control. The spiral happened when a thought affected my emotions and went to the pit of my stomach and made me feel worthless and inadequate. *I won't go there today.* With all this in mind, I told Rose to continue as I regained my composure and took another breath.

The first form was about education. Rose explained that my signature would allow the government to obtain all my records from the schools and universities I had attended. I signed it.

The second form was about employment. Rose explained that the government would obtain information from all my past employers. I shivered and signed it, feeling exposed, almost naked.

The third release form was for medical health records. Rose explained that the government would obtain all my past health records from doctors and hospitals.

"Rose, I hate this," I said.

"I know this is very difficult for you."

My stomach turned as I felt the shame. I was nauseous as I signed the release and tears filled my eyes.

The fourth release form was for Revenue Canada. As Rose explained its purpose, tears fell down my cheeks. I felt violated—my privacy was being taken away from me. I said, "Every year I pay income tax and every year they say it's not enough...I am a single parent; they just take and take my money at the end of each year. And now they want me to sign this." I took another rattled breath and thought about my inherent rights as a First Nations woman. I should not pay taxes at all. I was just a red child, a little red child.

The fifth release form was for police records. As Rose explained the form, I became even more upset. "I knew this was going to be very difficult for you," Rose said. "The government does want to know who they are up against; they want to be sure before they go through the process." I signed, feeling insulted, violated, and degraded.

Just like the signing of the Treaties, I thought.

On the drive home, I thought, *My God, they really are going to investigate me. What worse can they do than they have already done? The paper process has just legally raped me. They are still in control, still violating and molesting me through the legal process. I won't let this process discourage me. I won't, and that is my choice.*

I almost drove into another car and I wanted to go beat that person up for driving badly. *Maybe I should kick the shit out of them!* I swore at other drivers on the way home. Road rage had always been an issue for me. I had tried many ways to get rid of it, but that day I didn't care, although I knew I had to calm down before I got home.

As soon as I was safely home, I called the Medicine Woman, who was happy for me. The children had homework to do, and we had a quiet, relaxing evening. In the middle of the night I had another nightmare. I woke up at three in the morning and stayed awake. I barely made it through the next day, I was so tired. The following nights I suffered from insomnia. The shortage of breath and the rattle in my chest made me tired, physically and emotionally. But I knew this would pass and it did.

THEY ALL LEAVE

CALM. I CRAVED CALM. I BECAME SILENT, INTROspective, and oftentimes brooding. Once more I was trapped in a spiderweb of suspicion constructed from my own fears. The more I tried to push it away, the more entangled I became. *Oh where are the normal days. Or am I just insane?* I wondered.

At work, I felt like a burnout. At home, I would stay on the couch. I didn't go out with my fun crazy friends anymore. I was isolating myself. I wanted to be alone with just my children and the quietness of my home. My family and friends encouraged me to get out and maybe meet someone, go on a date. But I didn't care about men. I was afraid to attract someone unhealthy again because that was my usual pattern. I said the same thing my mother used to say about her relationships with men: "I just clean them up, dress them up, and then they leave." And my mother would laugh.

I didn't like that about my mother sometimes. It was as if my mom were proud to have had so many men in her life. After all, the old people on the reserve called my mother "Elizabeth Taylor" all the time. My mother would laugh her loud laugh and her vibrant energy stood out. But I saw a sparkle in her eyes. My mother liked to be called Elizabeth Taylor. Some of the men my mother brought home were good, decent men. I liked the men who tried to be my stepdads. They attempted to establish a father-daughter relationship and treated me well. But they all left eventually.

So far, every man in my life had treated me badly, and now I was too afraid of my own emotions, tired of continuously re-experiencing the same emotions that never evolved into wisdom. It was exhausting. I was afraid the men I attracted like magnets were emotional terrorists.

I still had great difficulty dealing with the effects of the terrible abuse and accepting what had happened to me at school. It affected my sexual intimacy with anyone. Intimacy confused me as I desperately fought for control of my feelings. I became numb, and I often succumbed to fear, similar to the feelings when I was that little girl being sexually abused by the priest. Intimacy resulted in fear, a rage of panic, and anxiety, all of which became a part of me, coming and going throughout my orgasms. An orgasm, which was supposed to be a wonderful, pleasurable, and normal feeling, was not normal for me. I picked men who could not express true, intimate love, men who never made love to me, rather who sought me out for their pleasure only. I often wondered if I would ever know what it was like to experience true sexual intimacy through intercourse. *Where is the love in it,* I wondered?

My friend Dee's words stayed in my mind: "Myrtle, we are just their maids. I don't want to be anyone's maid." Dee and I had that in common—always seeking and finding men that were emotionally unavailable.

I sat on the couch, eating a bag of chips and getting fatter with each chip, asking myself, *How has genocidal love affected me in my past relationships? How does a woman stay in that type of relationship and settle for all of the terrorist tactics. Over time, the spirit disconnects and eventually falls victim to the abuse and isolation. I slide into the role of victim, only taking scraps of his attention. A smart, intelligent woman, afraid to be alone and feeling desperate.*

I knew women like me. They would stay in that energy, hoping he would change. That was me.

GENOCIDE GOT MY BROTHER

LIFE COULD BE ONE OF PLEASURE AND WELLNESS or hell or sickness. Sometimes it was wonderful to be alive and to feel every part of my body and my heart beating in peace and completeness. But sometimes all I could feel was the terror and pain in my soul. But I was starting to understand that I had to learn to live each breath to its fullness. *Have you listened to a breath today?* I asked myself.

I wrote these thoughts on a piece of pink paper, opened my drawer of notes, and put the pretty paper among all the others. Then I grabbed a green journal and began to write with a sense of righteousness and power. I felt the tears coming and wondered how many more tears had to be shed before it would be over.

Please don't hide anymore and don't protect the people who made you this way. Don't be silent anymore. You made you the way you are. You got help to be this way as the genocidal practice upon a nation is now in effect forever. But you have to stop blaming now. How can I not blame anymore?

I wrote out the word *genocide* and then looked in the dictionary for its definition:

> Genocide: the deliberate and systematic destruction of a racial, political, or cultural group.

Destruction of me. I was part of a culture. Where is it? A tribe once with a family where kinship was honoured, unwritten laws existed, a language more significant than English, trees untouched, ceremonies a part of life, change of life and second childhood existed and were honoured in a circle of life so accepted. Where is it?

Genocide almost got me. Genocide has my brother, who walks the streets talking to spirits and gods, picking up butts, eating out of garbage cans, asking for change so he can buy glue and sniff the genocidal effects away. He hasn't bathed for days and his leg is seeping poison, perhaps gangrene. He smells like a dead animal. The family gives him a home to live in, but he won't stay. The clothes and shoes bought for him, he will sell them. So easy to get a mental health warrant to have police pick him up off the street and take him to hospital but my brother can survive and talk a good talk to get himself released. He is smart, and he is aware of what he is doing. He is not stupid. How many times have they tried to save him from genocide, but he is living it. He is in the genocidal effects. Can't everyone see that? So, he walks the streets begging, as his leg drips rotten yellow pus. His pant leg is soaked with pus. He will call on holidays and have dinner with me. Yes, he knows the family's phone numbers. They clean him up and give him new clothes and shoes. He goes to the bathroom and sniffs his glue and leaves, staggering down the street… talking to spirits… talking to spirits beside him.

I had escaped genocide by just a smidge. All my relationships were genocidal. "There but for the grace of God I go," I would say after another failed relationship. Never would I criticize my brother because I understood. Just the other day I had stopped him on the street, "When are you going to stop being a victim? You break my heart, brother," I said.

They got me in the assimilation process, that famous buzzword. I was somewhat assimilated, because how else could I live? Maybe assimilation had saved me because I could survive in the white world and I could also survive on the rez. I took Nimosōm's words of advice: "Take the good and the best of both worlds and live. Leave the bad alone." But sometimes I felt half in and half out of both worlds, living an abstract life.

When I looked in the mirror I saw the faint brown freckles staring back at me. I smiled at my freckles, my sparkling beauty spots, as I kicked down that door to my memories.

Every day the nun had told me to pray for forgiveness in the chapel. "Pray for forgiveness for having those ugly marks on your face or you will burn in hell for it, you evil little Indian girl, you ugly stink savage!" I went to the chapel as I was ordered. I knelt and prayed, "Dear God, please forgive me for having these evil marks on my face. Please don't burn me in hell." But now I know that my freckles are not evil. They are part of what makes me Myrtle.

NO ONE TALKS ABOUT IT

MY LAWYER CALLED TO EXPLAIN ANOTHER PROcess that I might have to go through as part of my claim. "Mediation is part of this process," Rose explained, "and that is what the courts order first of all."

"What you mean is that I have to sit with them and discuss an agreement?" I was suddenly afraid. I told Rose I was fully aware of mediation because I had been through it with one of my divorces.

"Exactly. You're fortunate to know the process. If it doesn't work, then we go to court, which they don't want. It would be very embarrassing for them. You'll have lots of time to prepare—these things take a while."

But I went about my days during the following weeks and months with pressure hanging over my head. It was messing up my life and upsetting the balance all over again. The emotions, the nightmares! I might have to meet with the priest, the nun, and representatives of the government and the Church! I was once again filled with fear and anger, and I was tired all the time. I hated being angry!

The day is coming soon when I will have my day at the table. The red child is going to meet with the queen's representatives and the school who took care of the red children. I wonder if they will look me in the eye.

I wrote my thoughts on a piece of paper and put it away in the secret place where I kept all my scraps of paper and journals.

The Medicine Woman helped me face my fears. She gave me medicine to ease the stomach problems that were causing bloating. My whole body was infected and in pain. I developed cysts on my ovaries. My whole existence was out of balance, but the Medicine Woman continued to help me until I became well again.

I continued to drive my children to their sports activities, events, school, and to see their friends. We attended family events together and travelled to powwows and art shows. At my lowest point, I had accepted that I could never be around large crowds of people, but now I was sometimes able to do it, but only when I felt calm and comfortable.

One day I got in the car, all set to go to work. The car refused to start. I hit the steering wheel and yelled, "Damn it, damn it! What is this going to cost me to fix it?" I stepped on the gas pedal, begging the car to start but it still wouldn't go. "What the hell!" Just as I broke into tears, I realized I hadn't put the key in the ignition.

Oh my God. I'm insane! I had a laughing fit as I put the key in and drove to work. I was so happy that nothing was wrong with my car.

I called the Medicine Woman and told her, "Actually, I feel strong about it this time. Excited that it's coming to an end. I've had no nightmares or body feeling-memories."

"You sound different, your voice has changed, and you sound confident!" the Medicine Woman told me.

I realized I was not afraid to meet the people who were responsible for torturing me when I was a child. In fact, I was looking forward to the day. "I'll sit up straight and look them in the eye because I am no longer their 'red child.'"

But the mediation meeting did not take place. Three years passed after signing the four release forms, with many calls back and forth with my lawyer. And yet there was still no response from the Church or the government.

Finally, however, a date was set for an examination for discovery, although that was still a year away.

"What is this?" I asked.

Rose explained that the examination for discovery was not a pleasant process and that it could be very difficult to go through. Lawyers for the school and the government and the Church would be there to meet with us. The lawyers would examine closely all that had happened in the school. I would have to speak in detail of the abuse. Rose informed me that another lawyer's firm would handle the process for me, because it wasn't her area of expertise. She said they were very good at this and would do everything possible to make me comfortable.

I fell apart again. Strangers would be examining my life. The examination for discovery would determine if my claim was to proceed or not. The government lawyers would ask me questions about all that had happened to me in the school and afterward. I would be required to speak in detail about incidents and specify dates. My anxiety returned. The flashbacks, the smells, the paranoia, the difficulty at work and home, the shifts of emotions were so evident to me that I thought it was obvious to the world too. Now, however, I was more aware of all my senses, and I had the tools to cope with this in a very healthy way.

I called the Medicine Woman and my therapist for validation and to get their support through my anxiety and fears.

In the months leading up to the examination, I faced my high anxiety. Nightmares and insomnia kept me up some nights. There were relationship difficulties with my new fiancé. Yes, my new fiancé. I had finally met a good Indian man who met all the requirements on my checklist. I had something serious going on.

Isa and Craig had grown up and moved out, and I started driving by their homes, sometimes late at night, to see if they were home safe. I was stalking my own grown children. I also drove by their workplaces and called them many times during the day. One day they confronted me because they were worried. They said I was too overprotective, so I agreed to drive by only once in a while. My children knew I was going through a tough time and that it made me feel better to know they were safe.

What I did to my fiancé was cruel. Our relationship worsened as I began to experience moments of rage. I accused him of everything and became verbally and physically violent to him and to myself.

In one of my moments of rage, I found myself driving at top speed down the highway with my fiancé. He pleaded with me to slow down as I sped toward oncoming traffic. He was sure we would be killed. But all I could think of was getting back at him and making him pay for the abuse that others had put me through. I knew it didn't make sense, but I was crazy with rage.

"Come on, baby, sweetheart, pull over and park so we can talk."

I drove toward an oncoming semi and then swerved at the last minute to the shoulder of the highway. I played this game a few more times with the oncoming traffic. My fiancé hung on for his life.

"I hate you. You're a lying cheating asshole. Tell me you're sorry," I yelled at him.

He pleaded with me to stop. "Please, baby, I love you. Pull over and talk to me."

I thought that I really had him scared. I pulled over to the side of the road and he reached for the keys smiling, at me, kissing my cheek and my hand. When he had the keys in his hand, he yelled, "You fuckin' crazy bitch! You're trying to kill me!" I didn't argue. He was right. I turned my head and smiled. He drove us home in silence, and I fell asleep.

I knew what was happening and that I had to stop this destructive behaviour. This was not the real me. I had to connect with what I had learned about how to cope in a healthy way. Well, it didn't happen overnight, but it did get much better as I took more care of myself. I was able to let go of the turmoil inside me, and I became one with myself. I felt my spirit healing. I thought about the healing process and the commitment to change when a person begins their healing journey. Connecting with the spirit inevitably helps to develop a healthier relationship with self and, ultimately, to have a healthier relationship with God/Creator and loved ones. But not like the God I had met at the residential school.

But the anxiety came one night and I packed up and left my home and my fiancé. It was only after leaving that I realized that what I had was good, and that I was trying to run from this good life. I had a real, true, intimate relationship; but intimacy had previously been so violated, and it scared me. It felt so unreal, so foreign, that I ran from it.

MY LIFE IN THE COLONIZER'S HANDS

WHILE I WAITED FOR THE EXAMINATION FOR discovery, I continued with my art shows. I learned to juggle time and manage it more effectively. I attended a critical incident-management training workshop as part of my healing plan; it validated what I went through in the residential school and the after-effects like trauma and grief. The workshop's purpose was to help people cope with tragic losses resulting from sudden deaths. It provided me with more understanding about Wade's tragic death, and I wished that a workshop like this had been available to me and family when he died.

I had made it this far. Perhaps some final validation, some satisfaction, and maybe even closure would finally come to me. I didn't like the word *closure*. That would never be possible. It couldn't be. Many things would remain unresolved for people like me. But I had hope that things would get better for me.

Rose called to schedule a meeting with the new lawyer, Donna, who would help me through the examination for discovery. "She is the best; she is very understanding and will prepare you for the process," Rose explained. It made me nervous that a new lawyer would know everything about me.

Donna had my case file and was familiar with the details. My nervousness subsided somewhat because Donna was so polite and respectful at our first meeting.

"My job is to protect you," Donna told me. "I've done many of these examinations. When I receive a case like this, I study it and am consumed with it until the day of the examination for discovery."

I felt relieved and that I was in good hands.

I arrived in town the day before the examination was to take place. Donna took me to the boardroom of her office, and there on the table were two big binders containing details of my entire life: my education, my finances, my employment, my doctors' visits, and letters from my physicians.

Missing, however, were reports from two very important people who had been assisting me with my healing and wellness over the past nine years. The therapist's report was not there and neither were the records of my documented visits with the Medicine Woman. I couldn't find them. The Medicine Woman had written about the healing she provided for me. I could not find her records in the folder.

Donna told me to prepare a timeline of events from the time I was born until the present. I was not accustomed to relating to things in this manner, and when I tried to think and write my story in a linear way, I ran out of paper. Starting over, I drew a big circle and put my ages on it from birth to present. I wrote briefly under each year what I remembered, all the memories collected in my journals. It prepared me for the legal process. I saw my whole life on that circle and it gave me some focus and chronological order. The perspective helped me feel in control, and it prepared me for the questions that were to come. I called it my story, and referred to it as my weapon for defence.

I spent the whole day in that boardroom, reading the binders and creating my timeline in the circle. I still hadn't finished at 4:30 p.m. when the lawyer's office closed, so I went to my hotel room and worked into the night to complete it.

On the day of the examination for discovery, I was very nervous and thankful that I got to drive with my lawyer to the meeting.

In the room sat one other lawyer and one clerk. The lawyer introduced himself and the clerk, who would be taking the transcripts and recording the session. The lawyer began by asking me questions about my family. I felt as if I were being examined under a microscope. He was prying the information from me. He also had newspaper clippings about my art shows and my job. Using the circle I had prepared, he went back and forth, asking questions about different times in my life. It was confusing at times. My life bounced around in that room. I felt interrogated, violated, and not believed by this stranger. I was telling a complete stranger about my life! I had to share with him my intimacy issues, my employment, my education, my expenses, my doctors' visits, my private parts, my emotional, physical, spiritual, and mental state.

How violating and inhumane is that?

My imagination took me flying away to a place where I survived as a bird eating worms and bugs. Birds would eat dead animals on the road to stay alive. And I had to survive and face the world after this. I had to hold on to myself and do the best I could to get through this day.

I felt small and my voice changed to that of a little girl. I felt belittled and humiliated. I thought I saw the lawyer snicker behind his stare. But maybe he was just doing his job.

Donna took me for lunch during the hour-long break. As we walked down the street, I felt loss in this town I hated. This was the town where my son was murdered. I saw Wade in every young man I met. I had committed to him that I would see this struggle to the end. Wade had been so upset with the Church and the government for hurting his family. He had read my journals and he wanted to write something about it for a school assignment, so he interviewed me. He was going to describe what he went through as a result of the physical and emotional abuse...the abandonment...how it affected him when he was a little boy. But he didn't get the chance to write it.

Donna bought me soup and a biscuit. I wasn't hungry, but I was grateful. I told her that I felt like I needed to defend myself.

"It's okay, you don't have to defend yourself; everything that's happening in that room will be on record. You can take this opportunity to tell it all!" Donna said.

I asked Donna about her law career. "I always wanted to be a lawyer," I said. "But the year my son was killed I lost the dream. That was our dream. We were going to move wherever I was accepted for law school. I was applying everywhere. Now it feels like it's too late. I feel too old for school," I said.

"I started late! I changed careers," Donna said, and her story gave me hope. I also felt sick and tired of my sorry, painful life, all the tears, some crisis happening within me every damn day. I had become used to the chaos, welcomed it, breathed it, loathed it when it was present and missed it when it disappeared.

That afternoon I sat up straight as I heard my voice describing what the Father had done to me. The government lawyer asked me questions again and again. My life bounced around in the room again. The emotions were intense and attacked my body. Grief, filled with sadness and pain. I didn't want to feel the pain again. I talked calmly. I cried whenever I wanted to cry because my lawyer had said to let it out. It was as if someone else were crying, as if I weren't there at all, but I was trying to be as present as I could be.

I was glad I had brought extra aspirin because I felt a headache coming on. I wished there was a pill to stop the feelings of dirtiness, shame, and anger that surfaced as I told my story. My wounds were exposed. If only the government's lawyer could scratch them out. Why couldn't he do that? Just scratch the wounds out with his pen, like when a mistake occurs. My head, neck, stomach, and private parts—gone—no more wounds, just a very faint scar where they had once been. I looked for the dot in the wall. I wanted to feel safe but there was no time to focus on running away into a dot. I needed to concentrate, to tell my story. I had to stay in the room.

How many people must have died as a result of this genocidal, terrorizing pain? Is this how they felt before they put the rope around their necks? Is this how they felt before they took all the pills or shot too much into their veins? How many people are walking around with the pain, the wounds, the hopelessness? They are helpless because they have been taught to be helpless or find themselves stuck and can see no other way out. Is that a learned way to live? I struggled to concentrate as I was reminded that this was how I lived. That was me. But I was not going to be a victim anymore of pain or of any person. I vowed to change my thinking from this point on. I would stay in the pain that resulted from being at the residential school if I didn't face it head on, acknowledge it, and live as if it no longer controlled me. The choice was for a better life. And even though it was difficult along the way, it would still be a better life.

I always told my children to walk on this ground like they owned it and hold their heads up no matter what was happening in their lives. I learned, thanks to the Medicine Woman and my therapist, that there was no good or bad. These were labels I wore. They had been passed on from someone who taught me these labels. I had accepted someone else's beliefs and values. I was taught to label my feelings, my energy, and my emotions as good or bad. A wonderful energy was blocked and could not move. I was taught that my emotions—anger, loneliness, jealousy, fear, hurt, sadness, and frustration—were bad. I was taught to shut them down and not feel at all. I was taught that to feel was bad. Since then, I learned that it is good to feel, that there is no such thing as bad feelings, and I was able to draw on my awareness of positive energy. Now I can have it all, including the wonderful feeling of powerful healing energy.

The day of the examination for discovery was not "bad." It was tragic, inhumane, humiliating, shameful, but it was also the truth. It was wrong that the government could interrogate me. So very wrong! I was revictimized, my residential school trauma was repeated. The government had the control to examine and exploit me in order to discover whether or not I was a victim of their actions. The final outcome placed my pain on a grid scale to measure its severity and determine points for payment. A payment that was to be the settlement of my claim.

How long will it be this time? What will the compensation be? What am I worth? To what degree was I sexually molested, degraded, and physically beaten when I was seven years old? How many points do I get for that? The government has just put me through a process of measuring my pain. My entire life graded on a scale. How inhumane is that?

I burned with unanswered questions.

How ironic that I had learned from my therapist to measure my feelings on a scale and grade them when going through difficult flashbacks. I was able to choose how long that emotion would be present and where it could take me. Through this process, I learned how to control my emotions.

It sickened me that the government used a payment grid to measure the abuse. That same grid formula was like a template for all First Nations. Keeping us all the same, as if the abuse didn't matter. It was insensitive, destructive, and controlling. The delay was even more abusive, as now I had to wait for the government to decide what my payment would be.

I signed the agreement that resulted from the examination for discovery. What the government didn't know was how I had learned to live in my body. What they didn't realize was that the experiences I had had in my lifetime felt like a disease; that a part of me was impaired and never functioned normally, but I had learned to live with it.

The examination for discovery hearing ended at six in the evening. In closing, the government lawyer asked me, "Why did you wait so long?"

"Can you imagine? The process of filing this claim was very violating. I want to take back my dignity, honour, and spirit, my childhood and clean it, purify it, and cleanse the hurt. That is what I want. My signatures authorized the government to place my entire existence in a petri dish and examine it under a microscope. I had to allow myself to be intensely vulnerable. It was a beating, a molestation, and degradation all over again. Your process raped me again like the Father did and hit me where it hurt so much, just like the nun did. Your genocidal practice to kill me as an Indian did not work, but it wore me down. It almost killed me. The existence of four parts of me—mental, physical, emotional, and spiritual—was in stress and turmoil for the past eight years of your processing of this claim. I had difficulty finding a balance in my life, and the past six months has been extremely exhausting. I am a mother, and a grandmother. I want to enjoy the rest of my life in happiness and peace."

Donna commended me on my courage and said, "I am so sorry you had to relive the memories."

I thought about Yellow Dog Breast. *Where are you? Did you see this coming? You saw this for the future, but the leaders didn't listen. They signed the Treaties, the Treaties that were to last for as long as the sun shines, the grass grows, and the rivers flow.*

On the long drive back to my home on the rez, I felt relief. I had done well in that room. It had taken eight years for the claim to go through and arrive at the examination for discovery, and now they would make me wait again. But at least it was over and documented. I would just have to wait for the final decision, whenever it happened.

PART SIX

WHEN WILL IT END?

"MODEL A" MYRTLE

IN THE WEEKS THAT FOLLOWED THE EXAMINATION, I felt free, and a gentle calmness settled within me. Maybe I had just had to say it all for the record. Life was in bloom again, and spring had sprung. The nightmares came and went. The anxiety hit and left. The shifting was in high gear, but I noticed that it was not as intense or as much of a struggle as it used to be. It was mostly smooth sailing. Maybe this was normal life. I knew the memories would be back again, but I also knew I was okay.

Things changed suddenly a year later, when the government offered a new Alternative Dispute Resolution (ADR) package. I wondered how much it cost the government to administer this to First Nations people. The ADR application and accompanying guide were as thick as books.

I was horrified at the many questions asked, and I could not believe this was happening again. I asked myself, *Why couldn't someone do something? Didn't they know what was happening out there?*

I was upset when I talked to Donna. She told me that, as a result of the examination for discovery, there were twenty-four undertakings to amend the claim. The government wanted the claim to be amended. *Perhaps it is a stalling tactic,* I thought.

The government would not look at the claim until the undertakings were completed. In one, the government's lawyer suggested that Donna add a claim for compensation for the damage to my nose. But to do so, I would have to prove that the injury was inflicted by the nun. I needed to provide documents, medical records to prove I was hurt, that my nose was broken. I had been seven years old at the time, so how was I supposed to provide a document that proved my nose was damaged all those years ago? Nevertheless, I obtained a letter from one of my doctors that proved that the damage to my nose was a childhood injury. The government, however, would not accept my doctor's report. I had not initially asked for damages for my nose. It was not in my claim. But the whole process of trying to get that information, which was not in my request in the first place, stalled the claim even further.

I was offered the new ADR process. Next was the Independent Assessment Process, but I was not sure if I wanted to take that route, jump through more hoops, eight years after I first filed the claim against the Church and government. What was there to gain after all this? Should I take this offer of ADR? Did I even have a choice? Yet another process was replacing the examination for discovery process. *What?* I could not believe this was happening. Then there was the Common Experience Payment, which was another application process for First Nations people who had attended residential schools. It was to compensate for loss of culture, and it used a formula for an amount for each year of attending the school.

I had excellent lawyers to help me through this frustrating, inhumane legal process. It was not my lawyers' fault; it was the controlling process of the government. Was the queen holding everything up? I smiled at the thought. The lawyers waited for my decision. A month later, after many tears of frustration and after asking many questions, I agreed to the ADR package and met with Donna to sign the document.

New York. This was what I needed. Finally some fun, wonderful experiences after all the horrible things I had endured while filing the claim. New York was amazing! "I love New York!" I yelled. Everyone in the street looked at me, but I didn't care because no one knew me there.

My old friend Ty met me at the airport. He was the only Cree I knew who lived in New York, and I hadn't seen him in years. Ty still sounded the same, with his Cree accent like he was from up north. Ty loved New York, where he had met his wife, Nessa. They had been together for years now. I was anxious to meet Nessa, but first I wanted to see the site of the World Trade Center. When I reached the spot where the towers once stood, I felt something that I couldn't describe. I felt like putting tobacco down, but where? I was overwhelmed with emotion. Ty told me where they were when it happened. I said I had seen it on the news and cried all day.

We all had supper together, and I felt like I had known Nessa all my life. I fell in love with her. Now I understood why Ty had never returned from New York.

The next day I rode the double-decker tour bus four times, with my long hair blowing in the wind. I imagined that Spider-Man or Batman was going to show up between the high buildings. I was fascinated with New York and Times Square. I rode the ship to the Statue of Liberty, all the time hardly believing I was in New York. I met many people, but the language barrier frustrated me. Everyone thought I was Spanish and spoke to me in Spanish. I loved Chinatown and negotiated for everything I bought there; Nimosōm would have loved it.

One night I was trying to get back to my hotel and I got completely lost and ended up in New Jersey. There were many lost people in New York. Tourists, visitors like me. They followed one another and helped with directions. All I had to do was find people who were just as lost and confused as I was.

I eventually made it back to my hotel room. I could have stayed with Ty and Nessa, but I wanted to treat myself to a hotel room and, because I was meeting Nessa for the first time, I had wanted Nessa to be comfortable and not feel pressured by my presence. "The next time I come to New York," I told them, "I'll stay with you in Queens."

I loved Central Park. Nessa told me that she had been rollerblading since she was fifteen years old and that she spent a lot of time in the park. She and Ty showed me the locations of all the famous movie shoots. The whole park was familiar to me as I had seen it many times while watching *Serendipity*, my favourite movie.

We stopped for coffee on a café patio. "Oh my God, is that Slade and Jo?" I asked Nessa and Ty. They were on my favourite TV show, *The Real Housewives of Orange County*.

"I will go get them and introduce you," Nessa said.

"Don't, Nessa! Oh my God," I said, "they probably don't want to be bothered. Don't. Oh my God." I tried to stop her but she was already talking to Slade and Jo and pointing to me and waving for me to come over. I asked Ty if my face was red. He said yeah and laughed. I got up as Slade waved at me to come over. Slade asked me many questions about Craig, who was a local TV star in Canada. Finally, we took pictures together with me feeling shy, standing between Slade and Jo.

Later at my hotel room I checked my messages. There were ten from my ex-husband Blake, saying today was our wedding anniversary and asking me to please come back to the rez. "I'm sorry I hurt you," he said. The four other messages were from my eighty-year-old Aunt Verna, who was worried that I would be raped and murdered in the streets of New York. Aunt Verna said my mother was worried too. The next day I went to many art galleries and took Ty and Nessa out for dinner to celebrate our friendship.

It was a year before my lawyer informed me that my application had been accepted and approved through the ADR process and that, according to their formula, I fell under Model A, the highest rate or score for the abuse that had happened to me. I felt somewhat acknowledged that they believed me. Finally! Almost ten years later, it was done. I was now just waiting for the final closure, the final signature. Or so I thought...

There were more forms to sign to release information about my life, and to my disbelief they were the same forms I had filled out more than four years earlier in the examination for discovery process. I had to do them all over again, and then I had to wait to go to another hearing review. Once again, I felt violated. How must the Elders have felt as they went through this lengthy process? I felt sad and hurt for them. My anxiety went up and down, and my ability to cope was unbalanced. It took all my strength to self-prescribe a routine. I was constantly adjusting my many hats.

"I need routine, balance. I need to nurture myself, breathe, drink water, exercise. I need to laugh," I said to my friend Sandra. "Now that my children are grown up and living on their own, why is it that I'd rather be alone sometimes?"

Sandra had her own explanation and asked whether it had been a sacrifice for me to not be involved in a relationship.

We talked about how there was no time for a relationship when you're busy with a family and career. Sandra said that was the choice she had made for herself. When I told her about the shifting, she was confused. I thought everyone knew about shifting and how to change moods when meeting different people or just coping in general. But Sandra was totally unaware of it, as she had never endured childhood abuse. I tried to help her understand.

One night I woke up in the middle of the night and reached for a pen and paper: *Crap! Here I go again. Awoken from a nightmare, feeling violated and betrayed. Well, fuck you, you miserable ugly creeps. You can't hurt me with your sickness, your sick, unhealthy behaviours. You can't control me. You can't take my voice and you can't stop me from living. You can't take my spirit anymore. All these years I let you do this and you don't even know about me. Me, a poor lost one in that familiar place. I am such a fool. I accepted all your infections.*

I arranged to go for lunch with my good friend Linda, who's a therapist. I loved visiting her because we have what I call "God talks." I said when I called, "And bring God with you today."

Linda laughed, "Oh yes, He is with me and He is here with you too." We didn't see each other often but we caught up fast. Linda truly believed in God. God came first and without God in her life she had nothing. This is what she believed because God had lifted all her burdens and now she had joy and peace. I wanted what Linda had, which was her belief in something greater than herself. I wanted to believe all the time and to be this joyous, happy person, or at least be at peace with myself. I enjoyed being with Linda and listening to her stories, but I struggled with believing in her God.

THE LIST

"Hey, Pauline, what do you think of *Genocidal Love* for the title?" I had finally put all my writing together in a book, and it needed a good title. But maybe *Genocidal Love* was too depressing. "Do you think Oprah will read my book?" I asked Pauline. "Oprah can help us show the world what was done in the residential schools. What about Ellen?"

I watched *The Ellen DeGeneres Show* every day when I got home from work. Ellen made me feel somewhat normal.

Pauline looked up from her BlackBerry: "But Ellen is crazy!"

I laughed, "You don't feel normal when you watch her show?"

Pauline put her phone down and laughed, "Myrtle, you're nuts! Are you really finished the book?"

I thought that maybe my book could help someone else. Maybe there was someone like me out there. People need to know that the genocidal effects continue.

"By the way, I want Jennifer Lopez to play me in the movie," I laughed. "I know. What a silly thought. It's only a fantasy."

Pauline was quiet. Maybe she couldn't imagine my book becoming a movie, but then again she hadn't read it yet. Pauline thought I was really nutty sometimes, like insane. But she also knew I'd take risks and go after my dreams and succeed.

Pauline laughed as she reminded me about the No Name brand days. We had lived in poverty while going to university. We always bought No Name brand foods. Our cupboards were filled with yellow boxes. Once we got good jobs, we were proud of our cupboards full of brand name foods and products. We felt truly blessed.

Years ago on the rez, when women talked about "the change of life," we wondered why they called it that. Everyone on the rez knew when an older lady had her womb removed. Pauline and I hoped that would never happen to us. It didn't sound normal. Who could we ask about this change of life, and why was it necessary to have the womb removed?

"Isn't that a hysterectomy?" Pauline had asked as she started doing yoga stretches. She was a yoga fanatic. I had tried yoga once but ended up pulling a muscle in my neck. "When sex doesn't matter anymore." Pauline went into downward dog and I wondered if she ever looked in a mirror when she was in that pose.

"Why is everything always about sex with you?" I asked, giggling.

"Why are we talking about change of life when we are far from it? Just wait till you get all dry inside. That happens to older women from any race, in any culture," Pauline said.

I was confused. "Really? Let's google it."

Pauline laughed when I told her about an incident when I went to buy Advil at a twenty-four-hour drugstore. This handsome white guy smiled at me and said, "Hi, how are you?"

"I'm fine," I replied, feeling shy.

"That's great. So what are you doing tonight?"

"Me?" I glanced around quickly, blushing as my heart skipped.

"Excuse me, ma'am, I'm on my cell!" The man frowned and pointed to his earpiece. I was so embarrassed that I rushed to pay for my Advil, but when I got in my car I couldn't stop laughing.

"Don't you tell anyone!" I said to Pauline as we both laughed hysterically. "How was I supposed to know he was on the phone?"

"By the way, what do you think are the most famous lines an Indigenous man uses to pick up women?" asked Pauline. I remembered some, Pauline added more, and I wrote them down:

The Creator has brought us together for a reason.
I am a traditional man.
You are Creator's gift of love.

I have never felt this way before.
My ex-wife is crazy and still wants me.
You're the only one I ever truly loved.
Let's grow old together.
Please have my baby.
Aw, you remind me of my mom and I want you to hold me.
I'm a powwow singer, you know.
My treaty number is sixty-nine.
You would look good on top of me.

Pauline and I laughed. "Pauline, if you hear any more, text them to me." She finished doing child's pose and sat up in her meditation pose. Her eyes were closed. I threw a bottle of water at her and accidentally hit her on the chin.

Pauline didn't say anything as she held her chin.

I was straining to look serious. "Are you mad? Are you all right?" The silent laugh that was stuck in my chest, shaking my belly and chest, came out through my nose.

"Oh my God, Myrtle, why don't you just laugh out loud? At least laugh right!" Pauline screamed as we both burst into giggles, and Pauline took the bottle of water and threw it back at me.

At forty-five years old, I married again, and the whole experience was quite different. I met Dan through a friend, and we dated for a year. Two weddings took place at home on the rez: first, a beautiful traditional wedding in the morning performed by an Elder, and in the afternoon we were married by a minister. It was a beautiful day for me and Dan.

We laughed as we reminisced about my checklist. I didn't need it anymore because my husband accepts and enjoys everything about me, loves my grandkids, my grown children, and even my mother. He loves my craziness and silliness. "Because," he says, "my God, Myrtle can give you the world! She can give you everything."

We listened to each other's frustrations, each allowing the other to vent about whatever was going on. Could this finally be happening to me? Dan was from a different culture and he treated me well and, most importantly, with respect. We laughed a lot together, loving each other completely.

I was amazed as I watched how beautifully my ten-year-old grandson danced the Grass Dance, which is a sacred dance blessing the ground and praying for people to be well. I felt blessed that he was my first-born grandson. He was a great hockey player in the winter and powwow dancer in the summer.

One day my grandson and I planned to go shopping right after work. I wanted to go home and change into casual clothes so I could be comfortable walking in the mall, but my grandson said, "Nōhkom, you will take too long. You don't need to go change. You look good and I saw this old, old man your age, like really, really old and he was looking at you in the store. You don't have to go change. That will take too long!"

I chuckled and reminded myself to call my daughter-in-law to tell her what her son said.

I loved visiting my grandsons. When my second grandson was seven years old, he told his mom, "I'm never going to church, only when someone dies. They give wine to kids! Wine! That man the priest said it's the blood of Christ. And bread, those li'l round bread? He said it's the body of Christ! But that's not the body of Christ! He's just saying that!"

I didn't want to laugh out loud; instead my heart filled with joy for the love and humour that filled my life; I was amazed at how expressive and articulate both my grandsons were, telling it like it is.

I waited three years for the government's response.

Finally the Independent Assessment Process hearing day arrived. My lawyer and her assistant prepared me before I met the adjudicator and the government representative. The adjudicator asked me questions, but she was gentle and didn't interrogate me like I thought she would. I even felt some trust, though it was difficult to imagine trusting another stranger.

I relived the trauma once again. I used all my coping mechanisms to keep my emotions in check. I felt the little girl inside me wanting to be heard, and I hurt. I felt dirty. I felt like a teenager again—a rebellious, angry, indignant, and stubborn girl was present in the room. I didn't want to talk back then, and I was angry all the time. I told the man, the government rep, that I hated him and then the adult woman in me took over, took control, and described what happened.

I felt the shame and humiliation all over again. *Regain composure; being abstract is okay,* I told myself.

I let the shifting move through numb, frozen, angry, hurt, and vulnerable, then to confident. I managed all the adjustments within me. I sobbed with the pain and the guilt of what I did to my children. As I spoke about the school, I smelled the foul stench; I stunk like that little ugly savage, the little ugly Indian girl. I asked them if they could smell the stink. They said no. I told them I was ugly. That the freckles on my face were the markings of the devil.

Later, the woman in me spoke and said, "I want to leave all of this here in this room. I want to get out of this cycle. I want this to be over now. I want you to acknowledge me and what was done to me. I want to speak my Cree language, I want to go back in time and nurture my children. I talk of the disassociation, the coping at work, at home. The cycle—and who said it ever goes away? It doesn't go away and it can't disappear. All the many therapy sessions cannot make it go away. But I take all the teachings to use and find what fits, what works. And I can control it. I learned how to do it and I continue to learn how to live with it as I adjust the shifts through the moments of the day."

At the end of the hearing, the government's lawyer spoke and validated and acknowledged all that I had said. I cried. I could not describe how I felt.

"Do you believe me?" I asked the government's lawyer.

"Yes, I believe you," he replied.

I was overwhelmed at that moment with so much emotion. It was amazing. It felt wonderful to let that energy go, and I cried and sobbed for what I hoped was the last time.

The day of testimony started at nine in the morning and ended at three in the afternoon. *This better be it for me,* I thought as I drove home. *This better be the end of this molestation, raping claim process, this violating and humiliating claim!*

I cried all the way home. The whole day went spinning through my mind. I hurt deep inside my heart. I took four deep breaths and drank more water. I listened to my music and felt better, though still emotional. I knew this process, as lengthy as it was, had helped my healing somehow. *How have I survived this?*

That morning my husband had called me to say, "Myrtle, leave it there, leave it all there. Don't bring it home." Maybe this time it would stay there because I felt really heard for the first time. This time they really listened to my story and believed me.

WE ARE ROYALTY TOO

August 8. It was my son Wade's birthday. He would have been twenty-five years old today if he were alive. It was also the day I got a call from my lawyer's office; the decision was in and the offer was there. Of course, they couldn't tell me what the offer of settlement was. I was to meet with them on August 18. I put Wade's picture on the table, wished him happy birthday, and put out offerings of tobacco, a cigarette, and some smudge. I also wrote him a letter.

My dear handsome beautiful son, my Wade.

I miss you tremendously at times. I long for you to be here. But I know you're happy and you're okay. You never wanted me to be hurt or cry. I was told by the old people that you want me to be happy and to live on in this life.

You would be twenty-five years old today. My first born, I love you so much. My heart will always feel you and hold you. I just want you to know that we are all okay. Your sister and brother are okay. Every year we celebrate your birthday. Every year we celebrate your life that was here and share your favourite foods. I miss you always. I wonder if you hear me when I talk to you out loud. Sometimes it's funny.

Sending you heavenly hugs and heavenly love my son. Hope you're enjoying your times with the Nōhkoms and Nimosōms in the spirit world. Tell them hello from me.

Momma will never stop loving you. Someday we will all be together.

Mom

My car broke down just when I had to see the lawyer for the final settlement compensation. I asked my friend Tess to drive me, and I promised not to talk about myself on the way there. Tess laughed, "That is the best part of our trip, your talking. It makes the drive go faster." I didn't know if that was a good thing or not, but I was grateful that Tess was ready to help.

When I finally arrived at my lawyer's office, Donna said, "Myrtle, do you want to read this over by yourself or do you want me to read it through?"

"You read it. I am too nervous about the decision." I could hardly sit still as Donna read out the decision and went through it so that I understood. The report was clearly detailed by the adjudicator. It was amazing!

As Donna read the decision, tears rolled down my cheeks; I felt sad for that little girl, for all that had happened to her in the school. The adjudicator had rated and scored my experiences with points. I could measure the harm that was done to me. And yes, my suffering and pain was acknowledged and given the maximum points. My lawyer said that this was the highest score she had ever seen.

The decision was made on behalf of both the Government of Canada and the Church. They were each supposed to come up with half the compensation. But who knew when the Church would pay their share; the decision had been made for them. My lawyers hadn't heard back from the Church. Maybe I would be able to end this horrific ordeal. Or maybe not. I had waited eleven years for this decision. No amount of financial compensation could replace what I had lost or fix the genocidal effects. But at least my voice had been heard.

Donna had a gift for me. It was a painting of beautiful colours in abstract designs. I tried to find words to say thank you—for the painting and for everything else.

When he was in high school, Craig had been chosen to show Prince Charles, the queen's son, around the high school and take him to events in the city. I made Craig a ribbon shirt that he had designed. I smiled proudly at the photos of my son and Prince Charles at the school basketball game. If only Nimosōm could see his great-grandson, his Cāpān, being chums with Prince Charles. Royalty walking with royalty.

Years later, my eldest Nosisim (*grandson*) danced before Prince Charles and his wife, Camilla, to welcome them. It was an honour. They shook hands with my grandson. My son had shown Prince Charles around the city and now his son was dancing in his beautiful regalia for Prince Charles and Camilla. I thought of Nimosōm again. If only he could see his Cāpān, my eldest Nosisim, dance, Royalty dancing before royalty.

Years later at a Treaty Four Gathering, my youngest Nosisim spoke to His Excellency the Right Honourable David Johnston, the Governor General of Canada. The queen's representative. He opened the event with an incredible speech. If only Nimosōm could hear his great-great-grandson, his Cāpān, speak to the queen's representative. Royalty talking to royalty.

My eyes filled with tears as I reread his speech. My youngest Nosisim, who was twelve years old when he presented his speech, reminded me so much of Nimosōm.

This is his speech:

> It is a wonderful honour to be here and meet you Your Excellency Sir David Johnston. Welcome to Treaty Four Territory. I would also like to acknowledge our honourable Chiefs, Elders, women, men, youth, and children here today.
>
> Let me start with a short story as to how I've become interested in the Treaties.
>
> Back when I was five years old, Nōhkom took me to Treaty Day on our First Nation. I had no clue what was going

on, all I knew was that I'd be collecting money because my ancestors had made an agreement in 1874, 142 years ago. That day I collected five dollars and I got upset. I threw the money in the air, kicked it, and shouted, "This deal sucks!"

From age five to twelve I have educated myself, I've asked questions, and this is what I know now.

In 1874 a deal, an agreement, a Treaty was made with the queen and the Indigenous people that she would provide hunting and fishing rights, health and wellness, education, and payment of five dollars per year. All this in exchange for our land.

Today these promises that were made in the Treaty are still provided to us as Treaty people. Only we are not covered 100 percent. My mom still has to top up when I get new glasses, which I'm only allowed to pick out every two years. My mom still has to pay for dental checkups and work extra hours. If I need braces in the future, my mom would probably have to save up or take out a loan... If I'm sick, my mom has to use her health benefits from work to cover extra costs of prescription drugs if she chooses not to get the generic brand.

Again I'd like to say this deal is unfortunate. Times have changed and what's done is done! And this is a very important history for all of Canada. The spirit and intent of the Treaty was to provide for Indigenous people forever.

There is a story in my family that my Cāpān's father, who is my great-great-grandfather, Anaskan, told many times and now it is passed on to us. That a man named Yellow Dog

Breast tried to stop the signing of this Treaty, but no one listened to him. He cried to the sky and threw off his robe and knelt on the ground and kissed the ground. He said, "This is my land." Maybe he saw what the future would be like.

If today, this moment, we were renegotiating that same Treaty, Your Excellency would be here on behalf of Her Majesty, the Queen meeting with our honourable Chiefs in this room. Communication and language would not be a barrier, and there would be a clear understanding of peace and friendship.

The five-dollar payment because of inflation would be thousands more today, perhaps in royalty payments each month to every Indigenous person. Medical and wellness would be made readily available for everyone. I would appreciate the coverage for my glasses every year instead of every two years. I'm growing and can't wear small glasses for two years.

Education for everyone that wishes to go to university, so they don't have to take out a student loan and have to pay it all back once they are successful. The coverage of funeral costs, as we are a dying population stuck in the past of broken promises, hence the residential schools that killed many little children and illnesses that cannot be treated without proper health care.

Treaties are fading, my people are suffering. We used to be rich, now we are poor. Whatever happened to the statement:

As long as the sun shines, grass grows, and the river flows…

The "spirit and intent" of the Treaties was founded on the belief that the Creator was witness to the Treaty negotiations and provided guidance through the Sacred Pipe Stem Ceremony. First Nations believe that, because the Creator was witness to this important event in their lives, all people involved, including the Crown and Dominion of Canada, would tell the truth and act in good faith with one another.

The spirit and intent of the Treaties. Promises will not be broken. Our lands of nutrients, medicines, food, and water in exchange for many promises. It is my hope that the spirit and intent of the Treaties will be there for me and many other Indigenous people; when I attend university for business and in the future for my children, grandchildren, and great-grandchildren, my Cāpāns.

The spirit and intent of the Treaties for as long as the sun shines, grass grows and the river flows…

Thank you for listening to me today and I hope you enjoy your time here in the beautiful Treaty Four Territory.

My grandchildren are precious and beautiful and the most joyful gift of life ever. I am grateful that my family continues to grow healthy and strong, living life to its fullest. I became a Nōhkom again for the third time when my baby granddaughter was born.

At sunrise, a Naming Ceremony was held for my eight-month-old granddaughter. My grandsons sat still and were excited for her because they already had their names and know who they are. The parents were happy. My husband worried, Nimosōm that he is, thinking his baby granddaughter might have a tantrum; it makes the hair stand up on his arms, she screams so loud. Surprisingly, she didn't scream. She sat very still through the ceremony as the song and the rattle sang her name. She peeked at them from under the cloth and smiled as if she knows. Tears came to my eyes, tears of joy and happiness for my beautiful little granddaughter.

Then along came another blessing: my fourth grandchild. Another granddaughter was born. At four years old, my youngest Nosisim, grand-girl, was in a naming ceremony before the sun came up one morning. It took a long time as she sat with her Quemay, the one who named her, listening to the songs and the rattle. We all sat together. She was patient, smiling as she peeked at us. It was a beautiful ceremony. When all was over my youngest Nosisim said to her mom and dad, "Are we going back to the world now?"

That night I wrote a note on clean white paper: *Yes, my family, this is our life; this is home, all of us with me and my Yellow Dog Breast. I'm absolutely sane. I'm abstract me. That is who I am. Me.* I tucked it in with all my other notes and placed it in the drawer.

Êkosi
(*That's all*, or *the end*.)

DISCUSSION QUESTIONS

Recommended for upper-year secondary school students (grades 11 and 12) and university students.

PRE-READING QUESTIONS

1. This is a fictionalized memoir. Why might the author choose to write a fictionalized memoir rather than a memoir? What are the possible pros and cons of this choice?
2. Look at the cover design. What do you think the image on the cover represents? Why do you think this design was chosen?
3. Consider the title of the book. Why do you think *Genocidal Love* was chosen? What clues does it give you about the book?
4. Do a KWL (Know Want Learn) chart of what you know about residential schools. Make sure to leave the (L)

column until after you have read the book. When you fill out the chart, consider these prompts:

a. What were Indian residential schools, and what do you know about their history in Canada?
b. How and why were the schools created?
c. What does the term *assimilation* mean?
d. What was taught at the Indian residential schools?
e. What were the roles of both the Church and the Canadian government in the running of residential schools?
f. How long did the schools last?
g. What do you know about intergenerational trauma?
h. How is intergenerational trauma created?
i. What do you know about the Truth and Reconciliation Commission of Canada?
j. What do you know about the claims process (such as the Alternative Dispute Resolution process and the Independent Assessment Process) surrounding residential schools?

PREFACE

1. What is the purpose of this preface?
2. Why is it important that residential school memoirs, including fictionalized ones, exist?

PROLOGUE

1. Why do you think the story of colonization is told as if it were a fairy tale? What is the impact of this choice?

What type of reaction do you have to hearing the stories of the Treaties told like this?

PART ONE: NŌHKOM AND NIMOSŌM

1. Why do you think the first part of the book is called "Nōhkom and Nimosōm?"
2. What does it mean that the powwows have become commercialized? (12)
3. Why do you think the story of Myrtle calling her mother a bitch was included? What did she learn from her punishment to have to stay home from the city trips? (16)
4. This first part of the narrative has a focus on eating and communal gatherings that involve sharing meals. An example can be found on page 16:

> Later that night a fancy meal was prepared. Potatoes, sausages, and spareribs were boiled in the same pot, tomatoes were sliced on to a plate, cream-style corn was put in a bowl, and sliced white bread was set on the table. The children each got a bag of chips, a bottle of warm Coke, and a chocolate bar to have after supper. Our grandparents loved to see us so happy.

What are some other examples in part one of communal gatherings or traditions that have a focus on sharing food or a meal? Why do you think the author chose to make this a focus of part one? What importance does this focus have for the rest of the memoir? Can you find any other examples in the rest of the text? How are they similar or different to the ones in part one?

5. On page 23, the book talks about family and ties of kinship:

> My mother told us that we came from a huge family on Nōhkom's side and were related to many families in the Treaty Territory; on Nimosōm's side we were related to many more families. She told us all the names of our relatives and explained the importance of family. "When you meet people," she explained, "let them know who you are and also your grandparents' names because your name tells a story of your kinship and family history. It is to keep the respect of kinship. It is so important to know who we are. It is an unwritten law.

   What other ways is kinship shown in the first part of the memoir? Think of examples that show family relationships that go beyond Nōhkom and Nimosōm. How is family shown through actions or words? How do these actions show family as a support system? How are these kinship roles important for the rest of the narrative?

6. What is the symbolism of the Sears wish book ending up in the toilet? (28)

7. How does Myrtle describe her home? Give examples of words or phrases that she uses. How does the description change throughout the story?

PART TWO: LEARN THE GOOD AND LEAVE THE BAD

1. What do you think Nimosōm's feelings are when he talks about the two worlds? Does he share his granddaughter's excitement? Does Myrtle pick up on his feelings? Are his words a form of resistance? (43)
2. Put the phrase "Learn all the good, leave the bad" in your own words.
3. What do you think Myrtle's feelings towards her first day of school are?
4. What is your reaction to the description of the nun:

> When my family and I arrived, a black and white thing appeared and walked toward us. It was a woman in a long black and white dress that covered her head; her face was very white and she wore round wire glasses. A black necklace with a cross hung around her neck. "Hello," she said, "my name is Sister." I thought she might be the queen's sister. (52)

Why do you think the author chose to describe the nun like this? Does it show the childlike nature of the narrator or the fear of the unknown? What feelings does this description evoke?

5. Why did the nun throw out Myrtle's new clothing? What does the loss of the clothing symbolize to Myrtle? (53)
6. In the first part of the narrative, we learn that Myrtle's hair is sacred and that she should not let anyone cut it. We also learn that there are traditions and ceremony that surround Myrtle's hair. When Myrtle's hair is cut by her Nimosōm, they save the trimmings in a bag and then burn the bag when it is full. (18) One of the first things that happens when Myrtle arrives at the residential school is that her hair is cut off by the nun who tells her, "You are shameful; your hair is full of bugs." (54) Why is this event traumatic for Myrtle? Discuss the emotions that you think Myrtle is feeling right now. What has she lost in this haircut?
7. List the ways the physical building of the school is described. Compare this to the descriptions of home from the first part of the narrative. How has the word choice changed? What do the descriptions reveal about the school?
8. The narrative transitions into the residential school experience very quickly. Why do you think this is?
9. This section that describes the residential school experience is very short in comparison to the rest of the narrative (only 16 pages). Why do you think there is more of a focus on the rest of Myrtle's life?
10. List the ways the children are described by the staff at the school. How do these descriptions evoke

stereotypical and colonial views? What colonial assumptions are they built upon?

11. How are the children and their self image affected by the way they are treated by the staff? Compare these two lines: I was confused about what *pagan* or *heathen* meant, but I knew that it was bad." (59) And "I still did not know what *pagan* or *heathen* meant, but I knew I must be bad." (60) What is the difference between the two lines? Why does Myrtle think that she must be bad?
12. What do you think life was like for children who attended residential schools? Provide examples to support your answer.
13. Many Christians see the symbol of the cross as representing love and forgiveness. How frightening would it be for someone who has never seen the crucifix before to be commanded to ask for forgiveness from it? Myrtle states, "In the chapel I knelt down and prayed for forgiveness for having the evil marks of the devil on my face. But I didn't know how to pray, and I was very frightened of the man nailed to the cross." (58) What other thoughts do you think are going through Myrtle's head?
14. Describe the differences between Indigenous spirituality that is highlighted in the first part of the book and the forced adoption of Christianity in this part of the book. Consider this passage from part one:

> When it rained Nimosōm prepared our home for prayer and smudged each room. Then he smudged

> the children with sweetgrass smudge. It was so comforting. The rumbling cracks of thunder came, and the rain showers followed. We felt safe in our grandparents' home as we listened to the thunder move across the sky. Our eyes grew huge at the sound of the thunder and we giggled together. Nimosōm talked about the thunderbird and how the bird's spirit protected us. I had a picture in my mind of huge, beautiful thunderbirds watching over our home. (19)

And this passage from part two:

> When all the girls were in bed and the lights were out, the nun said, "Hail Mary full of grace and Holy Mary mother of God, pray for us sinners . . ." over and over. It was scary listening to all the girls repeat these prayers in the dark. I wondered what it all meant, and I felt even more afraid as I lay in bed listening to everyone pray at the same time. It sounded so creepy. I wanted to go find Kaya but knew I couldn't. *I want to go home. Please Nōhkom and Nimosōm, come get me please. I want Nimosōm's prayers. I want his songs to put me to sleep and I want to hear his tapping to the songs on the kitchen table to put me to sleep. I want to hear his whispering whistle of songs at the table and taps on the table.* How I wished to hear Nimosōm's songs. Finally, with tears still staining my cheeks, I fell asleep. (57)

15. When Myrtle spills the milk from her bowl, the nun tells her to "Lick it up like a savage!" (62) What does this scene tell you about the way children were fed in residential schools? Do you think that the children are getting enough to eat? Give examples.
16. In the first part of the book, the importance of sharing food in a communal gathering is especially important. How is this act different once Myrtle is at the residential school?
17. How would you describe the curriculum of the school? What seems to be the primary focus of the teaching? What do you think the children learned? What did they learn about themselves?
18. Has the idea of home been tainted? How do you think Myrtle's life will change once she is out of residential school? Can things ever go back to the way they were?
19. Parts of this section are very graphic, and some people would say that they should not be in the book because of the graphic nature. What do you think? Why is it important for pages like this to be in the book? Do you agree or disagree with their inclusion?
20. Why do you think residential schools were operated in this manner? Why do you think they went on for as long as they did?
21. Why do you think that the staff of the residential school, apart from Miss Hart, are only called Sister or Father?

PART THREE: WHERE IS HOME

1. What do you think is the significance of the title of Part Three: “Where is Home”? In Part One and Part Two we have seen two quite different descriptions of what home is. We have seen the two worlds that Myrtle has lived in. How do you think she will navigate finding a new meaning of home?
2. Myrtle is affected by the residential school even after she is taken home. How do we see the impact the school has left on life? What values or lessons have been instilled in her and how does she express them?
3. What are the effects of Myrtle’s behaviour on her family?
4. Do you think Myrtle’s writing is a way to “keep the good”? What type of validation does Myrtle need? How can she stop living in between two worlds? (75)
5. What is the significance of the line: “the name I carried was not my mine”? (82) What is the impact of Myrtle’s mother’s news on her? Why do you think Myrtle reacts the way she does?
6. What does Myrtle mean by “subtle racism”? What are examples in the text of subtle racism? Can you think of any real-world examples?
7. What do you think of the therapist’s advice that Myrtle and her healing process are “like an old building” because “[s]ome of the bricks are strong and can be restored?” (84) What would you have told Myrtle? Compare this advice to Myrtle’s metaphor that she was

like a puzzle. (86) They both mean similar things but the tone of each is different.

8. Discuss how the type of support from friends and family that Myrtle receives after Wade's death. How does Myrtle come to see these kinship bonds and their importance?

PART FOUR: NO QUICK FIX

1. This part of the narrative focuses on stories of Myrtle's relationships with men. Why do you think that these stories were selected? What does each relationship show about her? What does she learn and how does she grow from these relationships?
2. Why do you think Myrtle and Ava went to see the school before it was torn down? Why is it important for Myrtle to have someone there with her? (118–19)
3. Myrtle comments, "Father told me what he did to me was love." (120) How has Myrtle's past trauma affected her and how has it shaped her idea of what love is? How has it changed her perceptions of relationships?
4. On page 117, we see the first mention of "genocidal love" outside of the title and the preface. What do you think it means in this context? It is mentioned again on page 127 when Myrtle writes in her journal. How does this journal entry add to your understanding of what genocidal love is?
5. On page 129 Myrtle claims, "Damn it, this was my home." What was her journey to get to her home? Is

this "home" in the same way as depicted in the first part of the memoir?

6. Myrtle tells the Medicine Woman that when Bray wants to make love and she does not want to, Bray tells her, "I am not the priest, Myrtle." (120) Myrtle also comments that in her relationship with Blake he tells her, "Don't forget the unwritten laws when you do that to your body. There is a price to pay when you sexually please yourself." (136–37) Are Blake and Bray's words and actions the same as the priest's? How do you see these actions as being similar to the ones used in the residential school where Myrtle was made to feel unclean and ashamed?
7. Why do you think the story of the vibrators was included? Why is Myrtle hesitant to go shopping with her friends? What is meant by the "old nun mentality?" (135)
8. Discuss the humour in this part of the narrative. Think about the story of the nose hair trimmers. (137–38) How is humour used? Why is it included and what would be lost if the humor was taken out?
9. What is "emotional terrorism?" (138) Can you find examples in the text?
10. Why was the story of Vegas included? What doesn't stay in Vegas? What does Myrtle learn about herself in this event?
11. Why do you think we do not get to learn the name of the man that Myrtle meets in Vegas?

PART FIVE: THE CLAIM

1. How important is Myrtle's relationship with Rose and later Donna? Beyond being lawyers, what roles do these women play for Myrtle? What do you think is the most important thing they help Myrtle with?
2. Myrtle tells the Medicine Woman that she saved her from death, and the Medicine Woman replies: "You saved yourself, Myrtle." (154) How did Myrtle save herself from death? Is this a turning point for Myrtle? How does she begin to recognize her own strength?
3. After the government responds with a document saying they are not guilty, Myrtle says, "I'm rejected and denied." (154) Why were both these words used? What is the difference between these two words? Is it only her claim that is rejected and denied?
4. How does Myrtle experience post-traumatic stress disorder (PTSD)? Does she always recognize it as PTSD? How does she learn to cope with it?
5. Discuss the comparison that Myrtle makes between the signing of the release forms to the signing of the Treaties. (160) How are they similar? How are they different?
6. What do you think/feel about Myrtle's choice to use the word *rape* to describe the process of signing the forms? Do you think this word is accurate for the situation? Why do you think that Myrtle uses this word? (160)
7. On page 164, Myrtle wonders to herself, "How has genocidal love affected me in my past relationships?" How would you answer this question if you were

Myrtle? Do you think that she has an answer to this question right now?

8. On page 166, Myrtle looks up the dictionary definition to the word *genocide*. How does she respond to the definition?
9. What is your reaction to the statement: "I escaped genocide by just a smidge"? (166)
10. What is assimilation? What do you think Myrtle means when she says, "Maybe assimilation had saved me because I could survive in the white world and I could also survive on the rez?" (167)
11. Both Donna and the government lawyers must study the case file and learn the details of Myrtle's life. Is there a difference between Donna's approach and the government's approach?
12. Why is it important that Donna tells Myrtle that she does not have to defend herself? (179)
13. Eventually, Myrtle accepts that she must see the world as having no good or bad. (181) Do you think that contradicts what her Nimosōm tried to teach her, or is this exactly the lesson that he hoped she would learn?
14. Analyse Myrtle's response to the government's lawyers' question of why she waited so long to come forward. Why do you think the lawyer asked her this question?

PART SIX: WHEN WILL IT END?

1. What do you think of the "'Model A' Myrtle" chapter heading? What does it mean?

2. Myrtle talks about wanting to have the same belief in something greater than herself that her friend Linda finds in God. (193) Do you think Myrtle finds the higher power that she seeks in herself?
3. Why were the Indigenous pickup lines (197–98) included in this part of the narrative? How does humor work in this text?
4. When Myrtle prepares for the hearing for the Independent Assessment Process, she reflects on the feeling of her past and how trauma shaped it. She frames this reflection by talking about the feelings she had as a little girl and as a teenager. (200) Discuss these feelings that Myrtle describes. If these past Myrtles could talk to her today, what do you think they would say to Myrtle? What would Myrtle say to them?
5. During the hearing, Myrtle narrates, "Later, the woman in me spoke." (201) What does the voice of the woman say? Analyse her speech. What do you think is the main focus?
6. How does Myrtle react to the decision for the final compensation? (205) What is the most important part of the decision to her personally?
7. In the Preface of *Genocidal Love*, Bevann Fox states,

> Then, in 2005, after a lengthy, intrusive experience like my hero Myrtle experiences in this book, I, like many other survivors, accepted a cash settlement from the federal government for my traumatic residential

> school experience. I almost immediately regretted it. I had money, but almost no sense of justice being done. And I, like all the other survivors who accepted settlements, gave up the right to sue the government for any future compensation. (xxxii–xxxiii)

Do you think Myrtle feels the same way about her settlement? Provide evidence for your answer.

8. Analyse Myrtle's grandson's speech to the Governor General. (206–9) Do you feel that this speech helps the narrative come full circle from the teachings that Myrtle's Nimosōm tried to teach her in the first part of the book?
9. How do you think Myrtle answered her Nosism's question, "Are we going back to the world now?" (210)
10. In the last journal entry that readers see, Myrtle states, "I'm absolutely sane. I'm abstract me." (210) What does it mean for her to be abstract? How does this self-reflection connect to Myrtle's journey of healing and growth?
11. How is this story an act of resistance and reconciliation? Provide examples.
12. Discuss how Myrtle has changed throughout the book. What were the turning points or main events that helped make her who she is?

POST-READING QUESTIONS

1. Why do you think it is important to read the stories of residential school survivors?

2. What do you think the word *resistance* means? Can you find examples of it in Myrtle's story?
3. Do you think it should it be required that we include survivor stories in curriculum and that stories like Bevann's/Myrtle's be taught at all schools?
4. What did you learn about residential schools? Return to the KWL chart you made in the pre-reading questions and fill out the L column. Was there anything you were surprised to learn, or a correction to a previously held belief?
5. After finishing the book, return to your answer about the title in the pre-reading questions. Do you think the title is a good fit for the book? Why do you think this title was chosen?
6. The book was originally called *Abstract Love*. Why do you think the title was changed? Why do you think it was originally called *Abstract Love*?
7. After reading *Genocidal Love*, do you have any ideas on how you can contribute to the process of reconciliation? Discuss some of these ideas.
8. After reading *Genocidal Love*, go back through the text and find all the instances where Myrtle is writing. She often picks coloured paper or a non-traditional paper (such as a napkin) to record her story on. How do the colours or types of paper relate to what she is writing? Can you make an abstract art piece representing Myrtle's journey using the colours she discusses in the memoir?

ACKNOWLEDGEMENTS

Thank you for the short years you spent with us, my son Kelly Joe Delaney Toto. August 15, 1978, to November 23, 1997. You are forever in my heart, my son. It is peace and comfort knowing you are with your Cāpāns, Kōhkom, and Nimosōm in the spirit world.

Thank you to my grandparents, Nimosōm Gaston Anaskan and Nōhkom Myrtle Anaskan (Mateech). Thank you for your love, protection, guidance, knowledge, and teachings.

Thank you, my amazing children, Chasta and Justin, whom I love with all my heart. My beautiful grandchildren, my Nosisimak, Sincere, Robbie, Chenoa, Chenia, who bless my life with love. Robyn, my daughter-in-law, brings culture and beautiful dance into our lives. My son-in-law Robert's quietness and respect brings a balance to our homes.

Thank you my beautiful mother Hilda Mary Anaskan (Woman with a Loud Voice), who left us November 4, 2008.

Thank you, my role model, Aunty Bernadette Blind, for always reminding me with, "Never give up, Kiyam. Go on with your life."

Thank you to all my siblings: Kelly, Kendra, Baby Joey, Gerald, Freddy, Mark, Lana, Dorie, Janice, Crystal, Velda.

My sister-friends Pam Fox (Lovas), Vera Walsh (Mahingan), and Sarah Longman, my best friends through life. Thank you for friendship, acceptance, and love.

Thank you, Irene Young, for showing me another way of life through traditional healing and laughter.

Thank you to Chris Sorenson and Rob Kirk, for your professional guidance in healing and wellness. The healing techniques are incredible.

Gratitude to lawyers Merrilee Rasmussen, Helen Cotton, Buffy Rogers, and Jennifer Houser for your amazing insights, support, and encouragement, and also to Karen Flemming, legal assistant.

Thank you to my first amazing editing team, Christine Harrop and Danyta Kennedy, for your initial work on the book. Through many texts, emails, calls, reads, tweaks, you gave me the courage to finish when I wanted to give up.

Thank you to Grace Stanley, Bachelor of Arts, Cree Language Literacy, for your assistance with the Cree in this book.

Finally, thank you to the University of Regina Press team for publishing my story and especially for connecting me with Sarah Harvey, whose professional expertise in editing kept my voice on every page. Since our first contact, she expressed her concerns about me revisiting the trauma, when in fact it made me more resilient and content. Thank you, Sarah!

ABOUT THE AUTHOR

Bevann Fox is a member of Pasqua First Nation, originally from Piapot First Nation. In 2012 she received her Bachelor of Arts in Arts and Culture and in 2018 her Master in Business Administration, Leadership from University of Regina. In 2014 she was honoured with the YWCA Women of Distinction Award—Arts, Culture and Heritage. She is the founder, producer, and co-host of Access TV's *The Four* and also works as Manager for Community-Based Prevention at Yellow Thunderbird Lodge/YTCCFS (Yorkton Tribal Council Child Family Services). She is also a certified yoga teacher and an artist in sculpture and/or acrylics.